S0-BNK-847

Joanna froze, meeting glinting eyes that narrowed. Her heart somersaulted under the impact of his touch, his closeness. Every cell in her body was suddenly charged with a fierce awareness of Luc's potent male charisma.

His grip tightened for a painful moment, then relaxed.

But instead of letting her go, he drew her toward him. His face was set and intent, his eyes molten silver.

Something feverish and demanding stopped her from jerking backward, from saying anything. Helpless in a kind of reckless, fascinated thralldom, she forced herself to meet that fiercely intent gaze. In it she read passion, a desire that matched the desperate impulse she had no way of fighting.

He dropped his hands and took a step backward.

"A bit too soon—and very crass—to be making a move like that, surely?" he said in a voice so level it took her a second or two to register the meaning of his words. "After all, Tom's barely cold in his grave. You could make *some* pretense of missing him."

The flick of scorn in his last sentence lashed her like a whip.

All about the author…
Robyn Donald

Greetings! I'm often asked what made me decide to be a writer of romances. Well, it wasn't so much a decision as an inevitable conclusion. Growing up in a family of readers helped; after anxious calls from neighbors driving our dusty country road, my mother tried to persuade me to wait until I got home before I started reading the current library book, but the lure of those pages was always too strong.

Shortly after I started school I started whispering stories in the dark to my two sisters. Although most of those tales bore a remarkable resemblance to whatever book I was immersed in, there were times when a new idea would pop into my brain—my first experience of the joy of creativity.

Growing up in New Zealand, in the subtropical north, gave me a taste for romantic landscapes and exotic gardens. But it wasn't until I was in my mid-twenties that I read a Harlequin romance novel and realized that the country I love came alive when populated by strong, tough men and spirited women.

By then I was married and a working mother, but into my busy life I crammed hours of writing; my family has always been hugely supportive, even the various dogs who have slept on my feet and demanded that I take them for walks at inconvenient times. I learned my craft in those busy years, and when I finally plucked up enough courage to send off a manuscript, it was accepted. The only thing I can compare that excitement to is the delight of bearing a child.

Since then it's been a roller-coaster ride of fun and hard work and wonderful letters from fans. I see my readers as intelligent women who insist on accurate backgrounds as well as an intriguing love story, so I spend time researching as well as writing.

Other titles by Robyn Donald available in ebook:

Harlequin Presents® Extra

Robyn Donald

ISLAND OF SECRETS

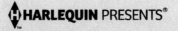

HARLEQUIN PRESENTS®

If you purchased this book without a cover you should be aware that this book is stolen property. It was reported as "unsold and destroyed" to the publisher, and neither the author nor the publisher has received any payment for this "stripped book."

Recycling programs
for this product may
not exist in your area.

ISBN-13: 978-0-373-23898-9

ISLAND OF SECRETS

Copyright © 2013 by Robyn Donald

All rights reserved. Except for use in any review, the reproduction or utilization of this work in whole or in part in any form by any electronic, mechanical or other means, now known or hereafter invented, including xerography, photocopying and recording, or in any information storage or retrieval system, is forbidden without the written permission of the publisher, Harlequin Enterprises Limited, 225 Duncan Mill Road, Don Mills, Ontario M3B 3K9, Canada.

This is a work of fiction. Names, characters, places and incidents are either the product of the author's imagination or are used fictitiously, and any resemblance to actual persons, living or dead, business establishments, events or locales is entirely coincidental.

This edition published by arrangement with Harlequin Books S.A.

For questions and comments about the quality of this book, please contact us at CustomerService@Harlequin.com.

® and TM are trademarks of Harlequin Enterprises Limited or its corporate affiliates. Trademarks indicated with ® are registered in the United States Patent and Trademark Office, the Canadian Trade Marks Office and in other countries.

HARLEQUIN®
™ www.Harlequin.com

Printed in U.S.A.

ISLAND OF SECRETS

CHAPTER ONE

IN A VOICE that iced through the solicitor's office, Luc MacAllister said, 'Perhaps you can explain why my stepfather insisted on this final condition.'

Bruce Keller resisted the urge to move uncomfortably in his chair. He'd warned Tom Henderson of the possible repercussions of his outrageous will, but his old friend had said with some satisfaction, 'It's time Luc learned that life can mean dealing with situations you can't control.'

In his forty years of discussing wills with bereaved families Bruce had occasionally been shocked, but he'd never felt threatened before. The familiar sound of the traffic in the street of the small New Zealand town faded as he met the hard grey eyes of Tom's stepson.

He squared his shoulders, warning himself to cool it. MacAllister's formidable self-possession was a legend. 'Tom didn't confide in me,' he said steadily.

The man on the other side of the desk looked down at the copy of the will before him. 'So he refused to give any reason for stipulating that before I attain complete control of Henderson Holdings and the Foundation, I must spend six months in the company of his—of Joanna Forman.'

'He refused to discuss it at all.'

MacAllister quoted from the will. '"Joanna Forman, who has been my companion for the past two years."' His mouth twisted. 'It wasn't like Tom to be so mealy-mouthed. By *companion* he presumably meant mistress.'

The solicitor felt a momentary pang of pity for the woman. Thanking his stars he was able to be truthful, he said austerely, 'All I know about her is that her aunt was your stepfather's housekeeper on Rotumea Island until she died. Joanna Forman cared for her during the three months before her death.'

'And then stayed on.'

The contempt in Luc's voice angered the solicitor, but he refrained from saying anything more.

Whatever role Joanna Forman had played in Henderson's life, she'd been important to him— so important he'd made sure she'd never want for anything else again, even though he'd known it would infuriate his formidable stepson.

MacAllister's broad shoulders lifted in a shrug that reminded the older man of Luc's mother, an elegant, aristocratic Frenchwoman. Although Bruce had met her only once he'd never forgotten her polished composure and what had seemed like a complete lack of warmth. She couldn't have been more different from Tom, a brash piratical New Zealander who'd grabbed the world by the neck and shaken it, enjoying himself enormously while setting up a world-wide organization in various forms of construction.

Bruce had done his best to convince Tom that this unexpected legacy was going to cause ructions, possibly even cause his will to be contested in court, but his friend had been completely determined.

Anyway, MacAllister had no reason to be so scornful. The solicitor could recall at least two rather public liaisons in his life.

A just man, Bruce accepted that a relationship between a sixty-year-old and a woman almost forty years younger was, to use his youngest granddaughter's terminology, *icky*. Involuntarily his mouth curved, only to vanish under another cold grey stare.

Luc said crisply, 'I don't find the situation at all amusing.'

In his driest tone, Bruce said, 'I realise this has been a shock to you. I did warn your step-father.'

'When did he finalise this will?'

'A year ago.'

MacAllister pushed the document away. 'Three years after he had that ischaemic stroke, and a year after this Forman woman moved in.'

'Yes. He took the precaution of having a thorough check—both physical and mental—before he signed it.'

In a clipped voice MacAllister said, 'Of course he did. On your recommendation, I assume.' Without waiting for an answer he went on, 'I won't be contesting the will—not even this final condition.'

The solicitor nodded. 'Sensible of you.'

MacAllister got to his feet, towering over the desk, his arctic gaze never leaving Bruce's face.

Bruce rose also, wondering why the man facing him seemed considerably taller than his height of a few inches over six feet.

Presence...

Luc MacAllister had it in spades.

MacAllister's lip curled. 'Presumably this

Forman woman will play along with Tom's condition.'

'She'd be extremely stupid not to,' Bruce felt compelled to point out. The other man's intimidating glance made him say bluntly, 'However difficult the situation, both you and she have a lot to gain by sticking to the terms Tom set out.'

In fact, Joanna Forman had the power to deprive Luc MacAllister of something he'd worked for all his adult life—complete control of Tom Henderson's vast empire.

Which was why the younger man's face looked as though it had been carved out of granite.

Once more MacAllister glanced down at the will. 'I assume you tried to persuade Tom not to do this.'

Bruce said crisply, 'He knew exactly what he wanted.'

'And like a good solicitor and an old friend, you've done your best to see that this is watertight.'

Luc didn't expect an answer. He'd get his legal team to go through the will with a fine-tooth comb, but Bruce Keller was a shrewd lawyer and a good one. He didn't expect to be able to challenge it.

He asked, 'Does Joanna Forman know of her good fortune yet?'

'Not yet. Tom insisted I tell her in person. I'm flying to Rotumea in three days.'

Luc reined in his temper. It was unfair to blame the solicitor for not preventing this outrageous condition. His stepfather was not a man to take advice, and once Tom had made up his mind he couldn't be swayed. He'd been a freebooter, his recklessness paying off more often than not until that tiny temporary stroke had messed around with his brain.

Which was the reason, Luc thought grimly, he and Joanna Forman would be forced to live in close proximity for the next six months.

Not only that, at the end of the six months she'd make the decision that would either hand him the reins of Tom's empire, or deprive him of everything he'd fought for these past years.

One thing he had to know. 'Will you tell her that she'll decide who controls Henderson's?'

And watched closely as the solicitor expostulated, 'You know I can't reveal that.'

Luc hid a bleak satisfaction. When required, Bruce Keller could produce a poker face, but Luc was prepared to bet that Tom had stipulated Joanna Forman not be told until it was time for her to make her decision.

Which gave him room to manoeuvre. 'And if her decision is against me, what will happen?'

Keller hesitated, then said, 'That's another thing I can't divulge.'

Well, it had been worth a try. Tom would have organised someone he trusted to take over, and Luc knew who that would be—Tom's nephew.

He'd fought Luc for supremacy in various overt and covert ways, culminating a year previously in his elopement and subsequent marriage to Luc's fiancée. Who just happened to be Tom's goddaughter.

Damn you, Tom.

Jo stood up from the desk and stretched, easing the ache between her shoulder blades. After two years in the tropical Pacific she was accustomed to heat and humidity, but today had left her exhausted.

The last thing she wanted to do was play gooseberry to a pair of honeymooners, but her oldest friend had brought her new husband to stay one night at Rotumea's expensive resort so her two favourite people could meet...

And Lindy and she had been best friends since they'd bonded on their first day at school in New Zealand, and it would be lovely to see her again.

Also, she was eager to meet the man who'd generated Lindy's rave reviews during the past year. A non-existent bank balance had prevented Jo from accepting her friend's request to be maid of honour, and the current recession meant there wasn't much chance of things improving financially for her for a while.

Not that she was going to dim the couple's happiness with any mention of her business worries. But the sooner she got home and made herself ready, the better.

Several hours later she realised she was wishing she'd made an excuse. The evening had started well; Lindy was radiant, her new husband charming and very appropriately besotted, and they'd sipped a champagne toast to the future as the sun dived suddenly beneath the horizon and twilight enfolded the island in a purple cloak shot with the silver dazzle of stars.

'You're so lucky,' Lindy had sighed. 'Rotumea has to be the most beautiful place in the world.'

Before she'd had a chance to do more than set down her glass, Jo heard a familiar smooth voice from behind, and the evening immediately lost its gloss.

'Hi, Jo-girl, how're things going?'

Jo froze. Of all the people on the island, Sean was the one she least wanted to see. Only a few days after Tom's death she'd refused his suggestion of an affair. His reaction had left her nauseated and furious.

However, she wasn't going to let his presence spoil the evening for her friends. She turned, wishing she'd chosen to wear something a little less revealing when Sean's gaze immediately dropped to her cleavage.

'Fine, thanks,' she said calmly, trying to convey that she didn't want him there without making it obvious to her companions.

Sean lifted his eyes to give the other two a practised smile. 'Hi. Let me guess—you're the honeymooners Jo's been looking forward to seeing, right? Enjoying your stay in the tropics?'

Seething, Jo wished she'd had the sense to realise what sort of man he was before she'd told him about Lindy.

Sure enough, her friend beamed at him. 'Loving everything about it.'

His smile broadened. 'I'm Sean Harvey.' Glancing at Jo, he drawled, 'A friend of Jo's.'

So of course Lindy invited him to sit down. Jo cast a harried look around the open-air restaurant, her gaze colliding with that of a man being seated at the next table.

Automatically she gave a brief smile. Not a

muscle in his hard, handsome face moved and, feeling as though he'd slapped her, Jo looked away.

Fair men usually looked amiable and casual—surfer-style. Well, not always, she admitted, the most recent James Bond incarnation springing to mind. In spite of the sun-bleached streaks in his ash-brown hair, this stranger had the same dangerous aura.

Surfer-style he was not…

Tall and powerfully muscled, good-looking in an uncompromising, chiselled fashion, he had eyes like cold grey lasers and a jaw that gave no quarter. He also looked familiar, although she knew she'd never seen him before.

Perhaps he *was* a film star? He wasn't the sort of man anyone would forget.

As though that moment of eye contact somehow forged a tenuous link between them, Jo's pulses picked up speed and she rapidly switched her gaze to Lindy.

Don't be an idiot, she told herself, and concentrated on ignoring the stranger and enduring the evening.

Not that she could fault Sean's behaviour; he was gallant with Lindy, man-to-man with her husband, and managed so well to indicate his interest in Jo that when he eventually left Lindy challenged her.

'You haven't mentioned him at all—is he your latest?'

'No,' Jo said shortly.

Her friend had spoken in a rare moment of general silence, and the man at the next table looked across at her. Again, no emotion showed in the sculpted features, yet for some reason an uneasy shiver skated across her skin.

All evening she'd been aware of him—almost as though his presence indicated some form of threat.

Oh, don't over-dramatise, she scoffed. The stranger didn't deserve it; she was still—unfairly—reacting to Sean's intrusions. Because of him she was totally off good-looking men.

For the rest of the evening she kept her gaze scrupulously away from the grey-eyed newcomer. But that sense of his presence stayed with her until she left the hotel and walked into the car park, stopping abruptly when a dark shadow detached itself from the side of her car.

'Hi, Jo.'

She froze, then forced herself to relax. On Rotumea the only danger came from nature—seasonal cyclones, drownings—or the very rare accident on the motor scooters that were everywhere on the roads. There had never been an assault that she was aware of.

Nevertheless, Sean's presence jolted her. She asked briskly, 'What do you want?'

This time he didn't bother smiling. 'I want to talk to you.'

Without changing her tone she answered, 'You said everything *I* needed to hear the last time we met.'

He shrugged. 'That's partly why we need to talk.' His voice altered. 'Jo, I'm sorry. If you hadn't turned me down so crudely, I wouldn't have lost it. I really thought I was in with a chance—after all, if old Tom had been able to keep you happy you wouldn't have made eyes at me.'

It wasn't the first time someone had assumed that Tom had been her lover, and each time it nauseated her. As for *making eyes*...

Jo reined in her indignation. Distastefully she said, 'As an apology that fails on all counts. Leave it, Sean. It doesn't matter.'

He took a step towards her. 'Was it worth it, Jo? No matter how much money he had, sleeping with an old man—he must have been at least forty years older than you—can't have been much fun. I hope he left you a decent amount in his will, although somehow I doubt it.' His voice thickened, and he took another step towards her. 'Did he? I believe billionaires are tight as hell when it comes to money—'

'That's enough!' she flashed, a little fear lending weight to her disgust. 'Stop right now.'

'Why should I? Everyone on Rotumea knows your mother was a call girl—'

'Don't you dare!' Her voice cut into his filthy insinuation. 'My mother was a model, and the two are not synonymous—if you understand what *that* means.'

Sean opened his mouth to speak, but swivelled around when another male voice entered the conversation, a crisp English accent investing the words with compelling authority.

'You heard her,' the man said. 'Calm down.'

Jo jerked around to face the man who'd sat at the next table as he finished brutally, 'Whatever you're offering, she doesn't want it. Get going.'

'Who the hell are you?' Sean demanded.

'A passing stranger.' His contempt strained Jo's nerves. 'I suggest you get into your vehicle and go.'

Sean started to bluster, stopping abruptly when the stranger said coolly, 'It's not the end of the world. Things have a habit of looking better a few weeks down the track, and no man's ever died just because a woman turned him down.'

'Thanks for nothing.' Sean's voice was surly.

He swung to Jo. 'OK, I'll go, but don't come running to me when you find yourself kicked out of Henderson's house. I bet anything you like he left everything to his family. Women like you are two a penny—'

'Just go, Sean,' she said tensely, struggling to keep the lid on her embarrassment and anger.

He left then, and when his footsteps had died away she dragged in a breath and said reluctantly, 'Thanks.'

'I suggest you let the next one down a bit more tactfully.' A caustic note in the stranger's voice was overlaid with boredom.

Jo caught back a terse rejoinder. In spite of his tone she was grateful for his interference. For a few moments she'd almost been afraid of Sean.

'I'll try to keep your advice in mind,' she said with scrupulous politeness, and got into her car.

Once on the road she grimaced. The spat with Sean had unsettled her; she'd totally misread the situation with him.

Like her he was a New Zealander, in Rotumea to manage the local branch of a fishing operation. Although from the first he'd made it clear he found her attractive, he'd appeared to accept the limits she put on their contact with good grace. Several times she'd searched her memory in case something she'd said or done had given him the idea that she wanted to be more than friendly. She could recall nothing, ever.

Frustrated, she swerved to avoid a bird afflicted with either a death wish or an unshakeable sense of its immortality. Naturally, the bird was a masked booby...the clown of the Pacific.

Concentrate, she told herself fiercely.

After Tom's death, Sean's suggestion of an affair had come out of the blue, but she'd let him down as gently as she could, only to be shocked and totally unprepared for his sneering anger and contempt.

She didn't like that he'd lain in wait for her to deliver that insulting apology. His belief that she and Tom were lovers still made her feel sick. It seemed that Sean believed any relationship between a man and a woman had to have a sexual base.

Neanderthal! In a way Tom was like the father she'd never known.

That night she slept badly, the thick humidity causing her to wonder if a cyclone was on its way. However, when she checked the weather forecast the following morning she was relieved to see that although one was heading across the Pacific, it would almost certainly miss Rotumea.

Then her shop manager rang to apologise because a family crisis meant she wouldn't be in

until after lunch, so Jo put aside the paperwork
that had built up over the month since Tom's
death, and went into the only town on the island
to take Savisi's place.

And of course she had to deal with the worst
customer she'd ever come across, an arrogant
little snip of about twenty whose clothes proclaimed far too much money and whose manners reminded Jo of an unpleasant animal—a
weasel, she decided sardonically, breathing a
sigh of relief when the girl swayed, all hips and
pout, out of the shop.

But at least Savisi arrived immediately after
midday to relieve her. She drove back to the
oasis of Tom's house, yet once she'd eaten lunch
she paced about restlessly, unable to draw any
comfort from its familiarity.

In the end, she decided a swim in the lagoon
would make her feel more human.

It certainly refreshed her, but not enough.
Wistfully eyeing the hammock slung from the
branch of one of the big overhanging trees, she
surrendered to temptation.

Her name, spoken in a deep male voice, woke
her with a start. Yawning, she peered resentfully
through her lashes at the figure of a tall man
with the tropical sun behind him. She couldn't

see his features, and although she recognised his voice she couldn't slot him into her life.

Groggy from sleep, she muttered, 'Go away.'

'I'm not going away. Wake up.'

The tone hit her like an icy shower. And the words were a direct order, with the implied suggestion of a threat. Indignant and irritated, she scrambled out of the hammock and pushed her mass of hair back to stare upwards, her dazed gaze slowly travelling over the stranger's features while she forced her brain into action.

Oh. The man from last night…

Feeling oddly vulnerable, she wished she'd chosen a bathing suit that covered more skin than this bikini.

Not that he was showing any interest in her body. That assessing stare was fixed on her face.

'What are you doing here?' she demanded. 'This is a private beach.'

'I know. I came to see you.'

Although Jo just managed to stop a dumb-founded gape, nothing could prevent her jerky step backwards. Shock, and a strange feverish thrill shot through her, dissipating when she re-alised who he had to be. Hastily she shoved on her sunglasses—a fragile shield against his pen-etrating survey—and blurted, 'You're the solicitor, right?' Frowning, she added, 'I thought you weren't coming until tomorrow.'

Not that he looked anything like a solicitor. Nothing so tame! Pirates came to mind, or Vikings—lethal and overwhelmingly male and almost barbaric. And very, very vital. It was hard to imagine him sitting behind a desk and drawing up wills…

'I am not the solicitor,' he said curtly.

Her eyes narrowed. 'Then who are you?'

'I'm Luc MacAllister.'

Like his face, the name was familiar, yet her groggy mind couldn't place it. Warily, she asked, 'All right, Luc MacAllister, what do you want?'

'I've told you—I came to see you.' Again he seemed bored.

Before she could organise her thoughts he spoke again, each word incisive and clear.

'My mother was Tom Henderson's wife.'

'Tom?' she said, everything suddenly clicking into place with ominous clarity. Heat stained her face.

So this large, brutally handsome man was Tom's stepson.

And he was angry.

OK, so after Sean's sneers last night Luc MacAllister probably believed she'd been Tom's lover. Even so, there was no need for that scathing survey.

Humiliation burned through her. It took a few seconds for pride to come to her aid, stiffening her backbone and lifting her chin sharply, and all the while, Luc MacAllister's gunmetal gaze drilled through her as though she were some repulsive insect.

An explanation could wait. This man was part of Tom's family. He'd taken over Tom's empire a few years previously, after Tom's slight illness. According to Tom, it hadn't been an amiable handing over of reins…

One glance at Luc MacAllister's arrogantly honed features made that entirely believable. Yet, although Tom had been manipulated away from the seat of power, he'd still seemed to trust and respect his stepson.

Fumbling for some control, Jo fell back on common courtesy and held out her hand. 'Of course. Tom spoke of you a lot. How do you do, Mr MacAllister.'

He looked at her as though she were mad, his grey gaze almost incredulous. At first she thought he was going to ignore her gesture, but after a moment that seemed to stretch out interminably, he took her hand.

Lightning ran up her arm as long steely fingers closed around hers, setting off a charge of electricity that exploded into heat in the pit of her stomach. Startled, she nearly jerked away. He gave her hand a brief, derisory shake before dropping it as though it had contaminated him.

All right, so possibly it hadn't been the most appropriate response on her part, but he was rude! And he couldn't have made it plainer that he'd swallowed Sean's vicious insinuation hook, line and sinker.

Disliking him intensely, she said crisply, 'I suppose you're here to talk about the house.'

Without waiting for an answer, she stooped to pick up her towel and draped it sarong fashion around her as she turned her back.

'This way,' she said over her shoulder, and led him through the grove of coconut palms.

Luc watched her sway ahead of him, assessing long legs and slender curves and lines, gilded arms and shoulders that gleamed in the shafts of sunlight, toffee-coloured hair tumbling in warm profusion down her back. Unwillingly his body responded with heady, primitive appreciation. Tom had good taste, he thought cynically; no wonder he'd fallen for such young, vibrantly sensuous flesh. Even in her prime, long before her death, his mother would never have matched this woman.

That thought should have stopped the stirrings of desire but not even contempt—now redirected at himself—could do anything to dampen the urgent hunger knotting his gut. He'd never lost his head over a woman, but for a moment he got a glimmer of the angry frustration that had driven the man last night to bail her up in the car park. She must have trampled right over his emotions...

But what else could you expect from a woman who'd chosen to sleep with a man old enough to be her grandfather? Generosity of spirit?

No, the only sort of generosity she'd be interested in would be the size of a man's bank balance—and how much of it might end up in hers.

Bleak irony tightened his mouth as the house came into view through the tall, sinuous trunks of the palms. One of these trees had killed Tom, its loosened fruit as dangerous as a cannon ball. He'd known the risk, of course, but he'd gone out in a cyclone after hearing what he thought were calls for help.

It had taken only one falling coconut to kill him instantly.

Luc dragged his gaze from the woman in front to survey Tom's bolthole. It couldn't have been a greater contrast to the other homes and apartments his stepfather owned around the globe, all decorated with his wife's exquisite taste.

A pavilion in tropical style flanked by wide verandas, its thatched pandanus roof was supported by the polished trunks of coconut palms. With no visible exterior walls, privacy was ensured by lush, exuberant plantings.

The woman ahead of him turned and gave a perfunctory smile. 'Welcome,' she said without warmth. 'Have you been here before?'

'Not lately.' In spite of the fabled beauty of the Pacific Islands, his mother had found them too hot, too humid and too primitive, and the society unsophisticated and boring. As well, the climate made her asthma much worse.

And once he'd retired Tom had made it clear that his island home was a refuge. Visitors—certainly his stepson—weren't welcome.

For obvious reasons, Luc thought on a flick of contempt. With Joanna Forman in residence Tom had needed no one else.

His answering nod as brief as her smile, he followed her into the house and looked around, taking in the bamboo furniture and clam shells, the drifts of mosquito netting casually looped back from the openings. A black and white pottery vase on the bamboo table was filled with ginger flowers in gaudy yellows and oranges that would have made his mother blink in shock. Although the blooms clashed with an assortment of brilliant foliage, whoever arranged them had an instinctive eye for colour and form.

Luc found himself wondering whether perhaps the casually effective simplicity of the house suited Tom better than the sophisticated perfection of his other homes...

Dismissing the foolish supposition, he said coolly, 'Very Pacific.'

Jo clamped her lips over a sharp retort. Tom had loved this place; in spite of his huge success he'd had no pretensions. The house was built to suit the lazy, languorous climate, its open walls allowing free entry to every cooling breeze.

It would be a shame if Tom's stepson turned out to be a snide, condescending snob.

Why should she care? Luc MacAllister meant nothing to her. Presumably he'd come to warn her she had to vacate the house; well, she'd expected that and made plans to move into a small flat in Rotumea's only town.

But Luc had bothered enough to defuse that awkward scene with Sean. And at least he was staying at the resort.

Still, she counted to five before she said levelly, 'This *is* the Pacific, and the house works very well here.'

'I'm sure it does.' He looked around. 'Is there a spare room?'

His dismissive tone scraped her already taut nerves. *No*, she thought furiously, you don't belong here! Go back to the resort where your sort stay...

Forcing her thoughts into some sort of order, she asked, 'Are you planning to stay *here*?'

He gave her a cynical smile. 'Of course. Why would I stay anywhere else?'

Sarcastic beast. Stiffly, she said, 'All right, I'll make up the bed for you.'

Dark brows lifted as he looked across the big central room to a white-painted lattice that made no attempt to hide the huge wrought-iron bedstead covered by the same brilliantly appliquéd quilting he'd noted on the cushions.

'Are there no walls at all in the place?' he asked abruptly.

Jo managed to stop herself from bristling. 'Houses here tend to be built without walls,' she told him. 'Privacy isn't an issue, of course—the local people wouldn't dream of coming without an invitation, and Tom never had guests.'

His black brows met. In a voice as cold as a shower of hail, he demanded, 'Where do you sleep?'

CHAPTER TWO

SOMETHING IN THE crystalline depths of Luc MacAllister's eyes sent uncomfortable prickles of sensation sizzling down Jo's spine. Trying to ignore them, she said shortly, 'My room's on the other side of the house.'

His frown indicated that he wasn't happy about that. Surely he didn't expect her to move out without notice? Well, it was his problem, not hers.

It would have been nice to be forewarned that he expected to stay, but this man didn't seem to do *nice*. So she said, 'I assume you won't mind sleeping in the bed Tom used?' And hoped he would mind. She wanted him to go back to the resort and stay there until he took his arrogant self off to whatever country he next honoured with his presence.

But he said, 'Of course not.' So much for hope.

She gave the conversation a sharp twist. 'I presume you flew in yesterday?'

'Yes.' Which meant he wouldn't be accustomed to the tropical humidity.

Good manners drove her to offer, 'Can I get you a drink? What would you like?'

Broad shoulders lifted slightly, sending another shimmering, tantalising sensation through her. Darn it, she didn't want to be so aware of him… Possibly he'd noticed her sneaky unexpected response because his reply came in an even more abrupt tone. 'Coffee, thank you. I'll bring in my bag.'

Jo nodded and walked into the kitchen. Of course coffee would be his drink of choice. Black and strong, probably—to stress that uber-macho personality. He didn't need to bother. She knew exactly the sort of man Luc MacAllister was. Tom hadn't spoken much about his family, but he'd said enough. And although he'd fought hard to keep control of his empire, he had once admitted that he could think of no one other than Luc to take his place. A person had to be special to win Tom's trust. And tough.

With an odd little shiver, she decided Luc MacAllister certainly fitted the bill.

If he preferred something alcoholic she'd show him the drinks cupboard and the bottle of Tom's favourite whisky—still almost full, just as he'd left it.

A swift pang of grief stung through her. Damn it, but she *missed* Tom. Her hand shook slightly, just enough to shower ground coffee onto the bench. In the couple of years since her aunt's death Jo had grown close to him. A great storyteller, he'd enjoyed making her laugh—and occasionally shocking her.

Biting her lip, she wiped up the coffee grounds. He'd been a constant part of her life on and off since childhood. Sometimes she wondered if he thought of her as a kind of stepdaughter.

When she'd used up her mother's legacy setting up a skincare business on Rotumea, he'd advanced her money to keep it going—on strictly businesslike terms—but even more valuable had been his interest in her progress and his helpful suggestions as she'd struggled to expand the business through exports.

A voice from behind made her start. 'That smells good.' One dark brow lifted as Luc MacAllister looked at the single mug she'd pulled down. 'Aren't you joining me?'

A refusal hovered on her lips but hospitality dictated only one answer. 'If you want me to,' she said quietly.

Following a moment of silence she swivelled, to meet a hooded, intent survey. A humourless smile curved the corners of a hard male mouth that hinted at considerable experience in…in all things, she thought hastily, trying to ignore the sensuous little thrill agitating her nerves.

'Why not?' His voice was harsh, almost abrupt before he turned away. 'I'll unpack.'

Strangely shaken, she finished her preparations. He'd probably prefer the shaded deck, so she carried the tray there and had just finished settling it onto the table when Luc MacAllister walked out.

He examined it with interest. 'Looks good,' he said laconically. 'Is that your baking?'

'Yes.' Jo busied herself pouring the coffee. She'd been right; he liked it black and full-flavoured, but unlike Tom he didn't demand that it snarl as it seethed out of the pot.

Sipping her own coffee gave her something to do while he demolished a slice of coconut cake and asked incisively penetrating questions about Rotumea and its society.

She knew why he was here. He'd come to tell her he was going to sell the house. Yet, in spite of his attitude, his arrival warmed her a little; she'd expected nothing more than a businesslike message ordering her to vacate the place. That he should come out of his way to tell her was as much a surprise as the letter from Tom's solicitor suggesting the meeting tomorrow.

Leaving the house would be saying goodbye to part of her heart. *Get on with it*, she mentally urged him as he set his cup down.

'That was excellent.' He leaned back into his chair and surveyed her, his grey gaze hooded.

It looked as though she'd have to broach the matter herself. Without preamble, she said, 'I can move out as soon as you like.'

His brows lifted. 'Why?'

Nonplussed, she answered, 'Well, I suppose you plan to sell this house.' He'd never shown any interest in the place, and his initial glance around had seemed to be tinged with snobbish contempt.

He paused before answering. 'No.' And paused again before adding, 'Not yet, anyway.'

'I wouldn't have thought—' She stopped.

He waited for her to finish, and when the silence had stretched too taut to be comfortable, he ordered with cool self-possession, 'Go on.'

She shrugged. 'This was *Tom's* dream.' Not Luc MacAllister's.

'So?'

The dismissive monosyllable sent her back a few years to the awkwardness of her teens. A spark of antagonism rallied her into giving him a smile that perhaps showed too many teeth before she parried smoothly, 'It doesn't seem like your sort of setting, but I do try not to make instant judgements of people I've only just met.'

'Eminently sensible of you,' he drawled, and abruptly changed the subject. 'How good is the Internet access here?'

'Surely you knew your father better than—'

'My stepfather,' he cut in, his voice flat and inflexible. 'My father was a Scotsman who died when I was three.'

In spite of the implied rejection of Tom's presence in his life, Jo felt a flash of kinship. Her father had died before she was born.

However, one glance at Luc's stony face expelled any sympathy. Quietly she said, 'There is access to broadband.' She indicated the screen that hid Tom's computer nook. 'Feel free.'

'Later. I noticed as I flew in that the island isn't huge, and there seems to be a road right around it. Why don't you show me the sights?'

Hoping she'd managed to hide her astonishment, she said, 'Yes, of course.' Her mouth twitched as she took in his long legs. 'Not on the scooter, though, I think.' Why on earth did he want to see Rotumea?

His angular face would never soften, but the smile he gave her radiated a charisma that almost sent her reeling. He was too astute not to understand its impact. No doubt it had charmed his way—backed by his keen intelligence and hard determination.

'Not on the scooter,' he agreed. 'I wouldn't enjoy riding with my knees hitting my chin at every bump in the road.'

Taken by surprise, she laughed. His brows rose and his face set, and she felt as though she'd been jolted by an electric shock.

So what was that for? Didn't he like having his minor jokes appreciated?

Black lashes hid his eyes a moment before he permitted himself another smile, this one marked by more than a hint of cynicism.

Sobering rapidly, Jo said, 'We'll take the four-wheeler.'

'What's a four-wheeler?'

Shrugging, she said, 'It's the local term for a four-wheel drive—a Land Rover, to be exact.'

An old Land Rover, showing the effects of years in the unkind climate of the tropics, but well maintained. Jo expected Luc to want to drive, but when she held out the keys he said casually, 'You know the local rules, I don't.'

Surprised, she got in behind the wheel. Even more surprised, she heard the door close decisively on her, penning her in. Her gaze followed him as he strode around the front of the vehicle, unwillingly appreciating his athletic male grace.

Once more that provocative awareness shivered along her nerves.

He was too much…too much man, she thought as he settled himself beside her. All the air seemed sucked out of the cab and as she hastily switched on the engine she scolded herself for behaving like a schoolgirl with a crush.

'Basically the road rules here amount to *don't run over anything*,' she explained, so accustomed to the sticking clutch she set the vehicle on its way without a jerk. 'Collisions are accompanied by a lot of drama, but traffic is so slow people seldom get hurt. If you cause any damage or run over a chicken or a pig, you apologise profusely and pay for it. And you always give way to any vehicle with children, especially if it's a motor scooter with children up behind.'

'They look extremely dangerous,' he said.

His voice indicated that he'd turned his head to survey her. Tiny beads of sweat sprang out at her temples. Hoping he hadn't noticed, she stared ahead, steering to miss the worst of the ruts along the drive.

She had to deliberately steady her voice to say, 'The local children seem to be born with the ability to ride pillion without falling off.'

Her reaction to Luc meant nothing.

Or very little. Her mother had explained the

dynamics of physical attraction to her when she'd suffered her first adolescent crush. And her own experience—limited but painful—had convinced Jo of her mother's accuracy.

She set her jaw. Sean's insinuations about her mother had hurt some deep inner part of her. Even in her forties, Ilona Forman's great beauty and style had made her a regular on the Parisian catwalks, and she'd been one great designer's inspiration for years.

To her surprise, the tour went off reasonably well. Jo was careful not to overstep the boundary of cool acquaintanceship, and Luc MacAllister matched her attitude. Nevertheless, tension wound her nerves tighter with each kilometre they travelled over Rotumea's fairly primitive road.

Luc's occasional comments indicated that the famous romance of the South Seas made little impression on him. Although, to be fair, he'd probably seen far more picturesque tropical islands than Rotumea.

Nevertheless she bristled a little when he observed, 'Tom once told me that many of the Rotumean people live much as their ancestors did.'

'More or less, I suppose. They have schools, of course, and a medical clinic, and a small tourist industry set up by Tom in partnership with the local people.'

'The resort.'

'Yes. Tom advised the tribal council to market to a wealthy clientele who'd enjoy a lazy holiday without insisting on designer shops and night-clubs. It's worked surprisingly well.'

Again she felt the impact of his gaze on her, and her palms grew damp on the steering wheel. She hurried on, 'Some islanders work at the resort, but most of them work the land and fish. They're fantastic gardeners and very skilled and knowledgeable fishermen.'

'And they're quite content to spend their lives in this perfect Pacific paradise.'

His tone raised her hackles. 'It never was perfect,' she said evenly. 'No matter how beautiful a place is, mankind doesn't seem to be able to live peacefully. A couple of hundred years ago the islanders all lived in fortified villages up on the heights and fought incessantly, tribe against tribe. It's not perfect now, of course, but it seems to work pretty well for most of them.'

'What about those who want more than fish and coconuts?'

She glanced at him, caught sight of his incisive profile—all angles apart from the curve of his mouth—and hastily looked back at the road.

So Tom hadn't taken him into his confidence—
and that seemed to indicate something rather
distant about their relationship.

'Tom set up scholarships with the help of the
local chiefs for kids who want to go on to higher
education.'

He nodded. 'Where do they go?'

'New Zealand mainly, although some have
studied further afield.' With the skill of long
practice she negotiated three hens that could see
no reason for the vehicle to claim right of way.

'Do they return?'

'Some do, and those who don't keep their
links, sending money back to their families.'

He said, 'So if you don't buy the tropical paradise thing, why are you here?'

'I came here because of my aunt,' she said
distantly. 'She was Tom's housekeeper, and insisted on staying on even after she contracted
cancer. Tom employed one of the island women
to help her, but after my mother died she asked
me to come up.'

He nodded. 'So you took her place after her
death.'

An ambiguous note in his voice made her hesitate before she answered. 'I suppose you could
say that.'

Tom hadn't employed her. He'd suggested she

stay on at Rotumea for a few months to get over her aunt's death, and once she'd become interested in starting her business he'd seen no reason for her to move out. He liked her company, he told her.

Luc MacAllister asked, 'Now that Tom's not here, how do you keep busy?'

'I run a small business.'

'Dealing with tourists?'

It was a reasonable assumption, yet for some reason she felt a stab of irritation. 'Partly.' The hotel used her range.

'What is this small business?' he drawled.

Pride warred with an illogical desire not to tell him. 'I source ingredients from the native plants and turn them into skincare products.'

And felt an ignoble amusement at the flash of surprise in the hard, handsome face. It vanished quickly and his voice was faintly amused when he asked, 'What made you decide to go into that?'

'The islanders' fabulous skin,' she told him calmly. 'They spend all day in the sun, and hours in the sea, yet they never use anything but the lotions handed down by their ancestors.'

'Good genes,' he observed.

His cool comment thinned her lips. Was he being deliberately dismissive? She suspected

Luc MacAllister didn't do anything without a purpose.

And that included passing comments.

Steadying her voice, she said, 'No doubt that helps, but they have the same skin problems people of European descent have—sunburn, eczema, rashes from allergies. They use particular plants to soothe them.'

'So you've copied their formulas.'

His tone was still neutral, but her skin tightened at the implication of exploitation, and she had to draw breath before saying, 'It's a joint venture.'

'Who provided the start-up money?'

It appeared to be nothing more than an idle question, yet swift antagonism forced her to bite back an astringent comment. Subduing it, she said politely, 'I don't know that that's any of your business.'

And kept her eyes fixed on the road ahead. Tension—thick and throbbing—grated across her nerves.

Until he drawled, 'If it was Tom's money I'm interested.'

'Of course,' she retorted, before closing her mouth on any more impetuous words. Silence filled the cab until she elaborated reluctantly, 'It was my money.'

Let him take that how he wanted. If Luc
MacAllister had any right to know, he'd find out
about Tom's subsequent loan to her from the solicitor—the man arriving tomorrow.

Was that why Luc had come to Rotumea? To
be told the contents of Tom's will?

Immediately she dismissed the idea. Luc was
Tom's heir, his chosen successor as well as his
stepson, so he'd already know.

Possibly Tom had mentioned her in his will;
he might even have cancelled her debt to him.
That would have been a kind gesture. And if he
hadn't—if Luc MacAllister inherited the debt—
she'd pay it off as quickly as she could.

A coolly decisive voice broke into her
thoughts. 'And are you making money on this
project?'

For brief moments her fingers clenched around
the steering wheel. For a second she toyed with
the idea of telling him again to mind his own
business, but it was a logical question, and if he
did inherit the debt he had a right to know.

However, he might not have.

'Yes,' she said, and turned off the tarseal onto
a narrow rutted road that led up into the jungle-
clad mountains in the centre of the island.

A quick glance revealed Luc was examining
a pawpaw plantation on his side. He didn't seem

fazed by the state of the road, the precipice to one side or the large pig that only slowly got up and made room for them.

'This is the area we're taking the material from now,' she said. 'Each sub-tribe sells me the rights to harvest from the plants on their land for three months every year. It works well; the plants have time to recover and even seem to flourish under the pruning.'

'How many people do you employ to do the harvesting?'

'It depends. The chiefs organise that.'

She stopped on the level patch of land where the road ended. 'There's a great view of this side of the island from here,' she said, and got out.

Luc followed suit, and again she was acutely aware of his height, and that intangible, potent authority that seemed to come from some power inside him. The sun-streaks in his hair gleamed a dusky gold; his colouring must have come from that Scottish father. The only inheritance from his French mother was the olive sheen to his skin.

Did that cold grey gaze ever warm and soften? It didn't seem likely, although she could imagine his eyes kindling in passion...

Firmly squelching an odd sensation in the pit of her stomach, she decided that from what she knew of him and the very little she'd seen of him, softness wasn't—and never would be— part of his emotional repertoire. It was difficult to imagine him showing tenderness, and any compassion would probably be intellectual, not from the heart.

So, after an hour or so you're an expert on him? she jeered mentally, aware of another embarrassing internal flutter. *Remember you're totally off good-looking men!*

Although *good-looking* was far too weak a word for Luc MacAllister's strong features and formidable air of authority. Composing herself, she began to point out the sights, showing him the breach in the reef that sheltered the lagoon from the ever-present pounding of the ocean waves.

'The only river on the island reaches the coast below us, and the fresh water stops the coral from forming across its exit,' she said in her best guidebook manner. 'The gap in the reef and the lagoon make a sort of harbour, the first landing place of the original settlers.'

Luc's downward glance set her heart racing, yet his voice was almost casual. 'Where did they come from, and when was that?'

Doggedly, she switched her attention back to the view below. 'Almost certainly they arrived from what's now French Polynesia, and the general opinion seems to be it was about fifteen hundred years ago.'

'They were magnificent seamen,' he observed, looking out to sea. 'They had to be, to set off into the unknown with only the stars and the clouds to guide them.'

The comment surprised her. Like all New Zealanders, she'd grown up with tales of those ancient sailors and their remarkable feats, but she remembered that Luc had been educated in England and France. She wouldn't have thought he had a romantic bone in his big, lithe body, and it was unlikely he'd been taught about the great outrigger canoes that had island-hopped across the Pacific, even travelling the vast distance to South America to return with the sweet potato the Maori from her homeland called kumara.

'Tough too,' he said, his eyes still fixed on the lagoon beneath them—a symphony of turquoise and intense blue bordered by glittering white beaches and the robust barrier of the reef. Immense and dangerous, the Pacific Ocean stretched far beyond the horizon.

'Very tough,' she agreed. 'And probably with a good reason for moving on each time.'

'They must have had guts and stamina and

tenacious determination, as well as the skill and knowledge to know where they were going.'

Yes, that sounded uncompromising and forceful—attributes as useful in the modern, high-powered world Luc moved in as they would have been for those ancient Polynesian voyagers.

'I'm sure they did,' she said. 'Over a period of about four thousand years they discovered almost every inhabitable island in the Pacific from Hawaii to New Zealand.'

She pointed out the coral *motu*—small white-ringed islets covered in coconut palms, green beads in the lacy fichu of foam that the breaking combers formed along the reef.

'When the first settlers landed there,' she told him, hoping her voice was more steady than her pulse, 'they didn't know whether there were any other people on Rotumea so they anchored the canoe in the lagoon, ready to take off if a hostile group approached.'

'But no one did.'

'No. It was uninhabited. Virgin territory.'

And for some humiliating reason her cheeks pinked. Hastily she kept her gaze out to sea and added, 'It must have been a huge relief. They'd have carried coconuts with them to plant, and kumara and taro, and the paper mulberry tree to make cloth. And of course they brought dogs and rats too.'

'You've obviously studied the history,' Luc said sardonically.

I don't like you, Jo thought sturdily. *Not one tiny bit. Not ever.*

Buoyed up by the thought, she turned and gave him a swift challenging smile. 'Of course,' she said in her sweetest tone. 'I find them fascinating, and it's only polite to know something of the history of the place, after all. And of the people. Don't you think so?'

'Oh, I agree entirely. Information is the lifeblood of modern business.'

Her heightened senses warned her that his words and the hard smile that accompanied them held something close to a threat.

Stop dramatising, she told herself decisively. He was just being sarcastic again.

Yet it was dangerously exhilarating to fence with him like this. Anyway, he'd soon leave Rotumea. After all, she thought irritably, there must be rulers all over the world desperate to speak to him about matters of national interest, earth-shattering decisions to be pondered, vast amounts of money to be made. Once he'd shaken the white sand and red volcanic soil of Rotumea from his elegantly shod feet, he'd never come back and she wouldn't have to deal with him again.

Cheered by this thought, she said, 'We'd better be going. I want to call in at the shop before it closes.'

And she hoped it bored the life out of him. She knew most men would rather chance their luck in shark-infested waters than walk into the softly scented, flower-filled shop that sold her products.

She turned to go back to the car, only to realise he'd done the same. Startled, she pulled away at the touch of his arm on hers, and to her chagrin her foot twisted on a stone, jerking her off balance.

Before she could draw breath strong hands clamped onto her shoulders and steadied her. Jo froze, meeting glinting eyes that narrowed. Her heart somersaulted under the impact of his touch, his closeness. Every cell in her body was suddenly charged with a fierce awareness of his potent male charisma.

His grip tightened for a painful moment, then relaxed.

But, instead of letting her go, he drew her towards him. His face was set and intent, his eyes molten silver.

Something feverish and demanding stopped

her from jerking backwards, from saying anything. Helpless in a kind of reckless, fascinated thraldom, she forced herself to meet that fiercely intent gaze. In it she read passion, and a desire that matched the desperate impulse she had no way of fighting.

No, something in her brain insisted desperately, but a more primal urge burnt away common sense, any innate protectiveness, and when his mouth came down on hers she went up in flames, the blood surging through her in response to the carnal craving summoned by his kiss. Her lashes fluttered down, giving every other sense free rein to savour the moment his mouth took hers.

He tasted purely male, clean and slightly salty, with a flavour that stimulated far more than her taste buds. The arms that held her against his powerful body were iron-hard, yet somehow made her feel infinitely secure. And mingling with the tropical fecundity of the rainforest around them was his scent. It breathed of arousal and a need that equalled the heat inside her. She wanted to accept and unleash that need, allow it to overcome the faint intimations of common sense, surrender completely...

And could not—*must* not...

Before she could pull away, he lifted his head.

Her lashes fluttered drowsily up, but when she saw his icily intimidating expression, all desire fled, overtaken by humiliation.

He dropped his hands and took a step backwards.

'A bit too soon—and very crass—to be making a move like that, surely?' he said in a voice so level it took her a second or two to register the meaning of his words. 'After all, Tom's barely cold in his grave. You could make *some* pretence of missing him.'

The flick of scorn in his last sentence lashed her like a whip.

Damn Sean's sleazy mind and foul mouth, she thought savagely.

But the brutal sarcasm effectively banished the desire that had roared up out of nowhere. Defiantly she angled her chin and forced herself to hold Luc's unsparing arctic gaze.

In a voice she struggled to hold steady, she said, 'Tom and I didn't have that sort of relationship.'

He shrugged. 'Spare me the details.'

'If you spare me your crass assumptions,' she flashed, green eyes glittering with some emotion.

After a charged pause, he nodded. 'I'm not interested in your relationship with Tom.'

He registered the slight easing of her tension. It seemed she was prepared to believe that.

Not that it was exactly the truth. For some reason the thought of her in Tom's bed sickened him.

But with a mother who'd made no secret of her affairs, Joanna Forman undoubtedly had an elastic attitude to morality.

As she'd just shown. Hell, she'd been more than willing. He could have laid her down on the grass and taken her.

Mentally cursing his unruly mind as it produced an image of her golden body beneath him, of losing herself in her carnal heat, he quenched his fierce hunger with the sardonic observation that possibly her response was faked.

Had she realised that giving away her lovely body might not be sensible at this time? Sex would mean she'd lose any bargaining power...

'For your information,' she said now, her tone crisp and clear, her eyes coldly green and very direct, 'when I was a child I spent quite a few of my holidays here, staying with Aunt Luisa. My mother travelled a lot, and Tom didn't mind me coming even when he was in residence.'

His brows lifted and she waited for some comment. None came, so she resumed, 'We always got on well.'

She stopped, then in an entirely different tone, the words a little thick as though fighting back a surge of grief, she finished, 'That's all there was to it.'

Cynically Luc applauded that final touch. She also made the whole scenario sound quite plausible; Tom had a history of mentoring promising talent.

However, he'd mentioned none of his other protégées in his will.

But her statement certainly fitted in with the information he had about her. She'd attended excellent private schools—paid for probably by the succession of rich lovers her mother had taken. However, she hadn't followed her mother's choice of career. At university, she'd taken a science degree and a lover, graduating from both just before Ilona Forman had developed the illness that eventually killed her.

Joanna had left a fairly menial job at a well-connected firm to care for her mother, and then found herself with an ill aunt who'd refused to leave Rotumea. Either she had a sense of responsibility for her family, such as it was, or she'd seen an opportunity to get closer to Tom and grabbed it.

No doubt it had seemed a good career move.

And it had paid off.

Luc let his gaze roam her face, unwillingly intrigued by the colour that tinged her beautiful skin. Perfect skin for a woman who made skincare products. Yet, in spite of that betraying blush, her black-lashed eyes were steady and completely unreadable.

Was she wondering if he accepted that her relationship with Tom involved nothing more than innocent pleasure in each other's company?

Tamping down a deep, unusual anger, he reminded himself that he had to live with her for the next six months. And that he needed her approval before he could assume full control of the Henderson organization.

You cunning old goat, Tom, he thought coldly, and held out his hand. 'Very well, we'll leave it at that.'

Surprised, Jo reluctantly put her hand in his. A rush of adrenalin coursed through her when long fingers closed around hers, a thrill that coalesced into a hot tug of sensation in the pit of her stomach. Her breath came faster through her lips, and she had to force herself not to jerk free of his touch.

OK, so he hadn't said he believed her. Why should she care?

Yet she did.

However, she wasn't going to waste time wondering about the reason.

But at the shop she was surprised. Tall and darkly dominant, Luc examined the fittings, and even took down and read the blurb on a package of her most expensive rehydrating cream.

She had to conquer a spasm of irritation at her manager's admiring glances. This was her domain, and he had no right to look so much in charge, she thought crossly, and immediately felt foolish for responding so unreasonably.

But something about Luc MacAllister made her unreasonable. Something more than his assumption about her and Tom. Something she didn't recognise, primal and dangerous and... and idiotic, she told herself bracingly.

Face it and get over it. He has a bewildering effect on you, but you can cope. He's not really interested in either you or your product, and you don't want him to be.

Back in the Land Rover, he commented, 'You need better packaging.'

She knew that. Though what made him an expert on packaging skincare products? 'That's all I can afford right now,' she said evenly, turning to take the track that led to Tom's house.

'You haven't considered getting a partner?'

'No.'

He said nothing, but she sensed his examination of her set profile as she negotiated the ruts. When she pulled up at the house he asked, 'And your reason?'

'I want to retain control,' she told him, switching off the engine and turning to meet his gaze with more than a hint of defiance.

His dark brows lifted, but he said, 'Fair enough. However, unless you're happy with your present turnover—' his tone indicated he considered that likely to be peanuts '—you're going to have to bite that bullet eventually.'

'Right now, I'm happy with the way things are going,' she told him, a steely note beneath her words.

When Tom had suggested exactly the same thing she'd refused his offer of a further loan without any of the odd sensation of dread that assailed her now.

Luc's kiss had changed things in a fundamental way she didn't want to face. His hooded eyes, the autocratic features that revealed no emotion and the taut line of his sensuous mouth—all combined to lift the hairs on her skin in a primitive display of awareness. He looked at her as though she was prey.

And that was ridiculous! He'd taken over Tom's huge empire, and had built it up even further. He was accustomed to organising and managing world-spanning enterprises. He wasn't interested in her piddling little business.

Or her, she thought, feeling slightly sick. There had been something about that kiss—something assessing, as though he'd been testing her reactions…

And, like a weak idiot, she'd gone up in flames for him. So now, of course, he'd be completely convinced that Sean's insulting accusation was the truth.

Well, she didn't care. Neither Sean nor Luc meant anything to her, and anyway, Luc would be gone as soon as he'd organised the sale of the house.

She said, 'I have no illusions about how far I can go.'

Without moving, he said, 'It sounds as though you're planning to stay in Rotumea for the rest of your life.'

She shrugged. 'Why not? Can you think of a better place to live?'

'Dreaming your days away in paradise?' he asked contemptuously.

CHAPTER THREE

'I PRESUME YOU have no idea of how patronising you sound.'

It didn't need the subtle ironic uplift of Luc's dark brows to make Jo regret she'd voiced her irritation.

How did that slight movement give his handsome face such a saturnine aspect?

But he said levelly, 'I didn't intend to be. Rotumea is a very small dot in a very empty ocean, a long way from anywhere. If your stuff's any good, don't you want to take it to the world?'

Torn, she hesitated, and saw the corners of his mouth lift, as though in expectation of a smile—a triumphant one.

Goaded, she said explosively, 'Not if it means handing over any control to anyone else. I have an arrangement with the local people and I value the ones who work with me—I feel I've established a business that takes their ambitions and needs seriously. I don't believe I'd be any happier if I were making megabucks and living in some designer penthouse in a huge, noisy, polluted city.' She paused, before finishing more calmly, 'And my product is better than good—it's *superb*.'

'If your skin is any indication of its effect, then I believe you.'

Delivered in a voice so dispassionate it took her a second to realise what he'd said, the compliment disturbed her. Uncertainly, she said, 'Thank you,' and opened the door of the Land Rover, stopping when he began to speak again.

'Although if you were making real money you could choose wherever you want to live,' he said coolly. 'Modern communications being as sophisticated as they are, no one has to live over the shop any more.'

'Agreed, but apart from liking Rotumea, in Polynesia personal relationships are important in business.'

Another lift of those dark brows. 'No doubt.'

After an undecided moment she ignored the distinctly sardonic note to his words. Instead she said, 'I like to keep a close watch on everything.'

Luc's nod was accompanied by a measuring glance. 'How to delegate is one of the lessons all entrepreneurs have to learn.' He looked at his watch. 'When do you eat at night? I assume I'll have to reserve a table for us at the resort.'

Relieved, Jo permitted herself a wry smile. She'd been wondering whether he'd expect her to cook for him. 'It's sensible to do so.' But something forced her to add, 'We don't have to go there if you don't want to. I'm actually quite a good cook. Basic, but the food's edible, Tom used to say.'

'I'm sure he didn't employ you for your prowess in the kitchen,' Luc said smoothly.

Something about his tone set her teeth on edge. She opened her mouth to tell him Tom hadn't employed her at all, then closed it again.

The arrangement she had with Tom was none of Luc's business, and anyway, he wouldn't believe her.

Taking her silence for agreement, he said, 'Then I'll reserve a table. Eight tonight?'

Jo hesitated, then nodded. 'Thank you,' she said and got out of the Land Rover.

Inside the house, she opened a wardrobe door and stared at its meagre contents. Her one good dinner dress had been aired the previous evening in honour of Lindy and her husband.

Of course it didn't matter what she chose. After all, she wasn't trying to impress anyone.

In the end she pulled on a cotton voile dress

that floated to her ankles, its pale yellow-green background printed in the gentle swirls of colour that suited her colouring. In her hair she tucked a gardenia flower.

Once ready, she examined her reflection critically. Yes, it looked good, fresh and tropical and casual—and not, she hoped, as though she'd gone to any trouble… Deliberately she'd kept her make-up low-key and simply combed her hair back from her face.

When she emerged from her room he was standing on the terrace but he turned immediately and gave her a cool, speculative survey.

'If you say I'm looking very Pacific,' she said before she could stop herself, 'I might start to think you have a bias against Pacific style.'

His smile was brief. 'Not guilty,' he said. 'You look charming, as I'm sure you know.'

'I intend to take that as a compliment,' she said coolly.

'It was meant to be.'

A compliment with a sting, she thought with a mental grimace.

It set the tone for the evening. Not that he was overtly antagonistic; in fact he was an excellent host. Before long she was laughing, and his conversation both stimulated and challenged her. If Luc had been any other man she'd have enjoyed the occasion, yet she had to keep telling herself to relax. She was far too conscious of his hard-edged control and the coolly unreadable composure that set every nerve jangling.

Too aware of the man himself.

And made uncomfortable by the covert observation of others in the restaurant. Especially the women casting envious looks her way.

Of course the resort advertising hinted at the possibility of a romantic experience, enticing guests with the allure of the tropics—the seductive, languorous perfume of frangipani and gardenia floating on the breeze that played lazily across bare skin, the promised glamour of a lover's moon rising over the reef.

And in spite of its exclusive guest list, tonight Luc was definitely the dominant male in the open-air lanai, radiating that indefinable thing called presence.

However, vitally masculine though he was, she wasn't interested in Luc MacAllister.

In any way, she told herself trenchantly.

So her reaction to those appreciative feminine glances bewildered her. A spiky, territorial instinct, it was an emotion she'd never felt before, and her unusual susceptibility sharpened her voice with a brittle, almost aggressive note.

Luc's voice broke into her thoughts. She looked

up, meeting his narrowed grey eyes with something close to defiance.

'Something wrong with the fish?' he drawled.

'Of course not,' she said swiftly, attacking it
with what she hoped looked like relish. It seemed
to lack flavour, as though by Luc's mere presence he overwhelmed any other sensory input.

And that was just plain ridiculous.

Thankfully the evening seemed to race by,
but the unusually significant tension that twisted
through her increased. By the time they returned
to the house she was so tense she flinched when
a blur of movement shot up from the sandy
ground as they walked the few steps from the
garage.

'It's only a bird,' Luc said, sounding surprised.

'I know.' She was being idiotic. Completely,
foolishly, *childishly* over the top—behaving like
an adolescent in the first throes of a crush.

She didn't even *like* Tom's stepson, she
thought resentfully, invoking Tom's name as
some sort of talisman while she showered in
the tiny bathroom off her room.

And he certainly didn't like her. He'd listened
to Sean's poison and chosen to believe it, convinced she was the sort of woman who'd sleep
with a man for money.

When he didn't even know her…

It hurt. Snorting at her stupidity, she turned off the unrefreshing lukewarm water and resolutely switched her mind to other things.

And failed. In bed she lay open-eyed, wooing sleep. For once the dull roar of the waves against the reef didn't work its usual soothing magic. Wild, baseless forebodings swirled through her head, playing havoc with her thoughts.

Eventually she slipped into a doze, waking to the sound of gulls squabbling on the beach and the gleam of the sun through the curtains. The angle of its rays told her it was well above the horizon.

Jerking upright, she glanced at her watch, gave a startled exclamation and leapt out of the bed.

In a couple of hours she had to be at the resort to meet the solicitor from New Zealand. The uneasy chill that tightened her skin was because the solicitor would probably tell her she had to pay back the loan Tom had made to her.

And that would be extremely difficult.

Actually, right now it would be impossible.

Every cent she possessed was invested in her business. She had already approached the small local branch of the bank, but after consulting his superiors on the main island the manager had indicated they weren't inclined to take over the loan.

Oh, Tom, she thought, aching with sudden grief, why did you have to die...?

She missed him so much. In his gruff, cynical way he'd taken the place of the father she'd never known.

Telling herself to toughen up, she raced through her morning rituals before walking into the kitchen. The house was as silent as it had been since Tom died, and even before she saw the note on the bench she knew Luc MacAllister wasn't in it.

She stood for a moment, looking down at the writing. Just as she'd have imagined it, she thought a little caustically. Bold and black and clear; a very incisive, businesslike—not to say forthright—hand.

It announced, *Back at eight a.m.* and was signed with his initials.

She crumpled it up and glanced at her watch again, then rummaged in the refrigerator. Most men his height and build probably ate a cooked breakfast, but this morning he could have the same as she did—cereals and a bowl of fruit— and if he needed more to fuel that big stream- lined body, there were eggs in the fridge for him to cook.

She ate breakfast too fast, decided against coffee and glanced again at her watch. Half an hour to fill. It stretched before her like an eternity. The sea always calmed her—perhaps it would work its magic now.

But her stomach remained a refuge for butterflies even after she'd walked through the sighing palms and stopped in the heavy shade of the trees lining this part of the beach. A towel on the sand drew her gaze out over the lagoon.

Sunlight glittered across the water, bestowing heat to the sand and weaving radiance through the great rollers as they dashed themselves in a fury of foam against the obstinate reef. On the calm waters inside its shelter, a small canoe carrying two boys danced its way down the coastline.

Squinting against the brilliance, Jo spotted Luc swimming towards the shore, powerful arms and shoulders moving easily, soundlessly through the warm waters. An unexpected heat banished the dark cloud of worry; her breath locked in her lungs as he stood up, water streaming down to emphasise bronzed shoulders and chest and long, strongly muscled legs.

For such a sophisticated man he looked magnificently physical, like some ancient god of the sea—compelling and charismatic as he strode towards the shore.

Startled by a fierce stab of sensation in every nerve, her senses on full alert, Jo looked away and pretended to watch the little canoe darting across the water. It seemed intrusive to stare at Luc when he had no knowledge of her presence and she disliked feeling like a voyeur.

Her stomach clenched with a different sort of apprehension as he came closer. She stiffened her shoulders, turning to face a survey that held a cool enquiry. Every traitorous nerve in her body tightened in a brief, shocking acknowledgement of his compelling male magnetism.

Without smiling, Luc nodded and said briefly, 'Good morning.'

At least he hadn't noticed her wildfire reaction. She returned the greeting, her mouth drying when he stooped and picked up his towel. How on earth had he developed the muscles so lovingly highlighted by the sun?

Working out, she told herself prosaically, adding a wry addendum, *Lots and lots of it.* And weights. Very heavy weights...

After drying his face he said, 'Kind of you to come down, but I could have found my way back.'

'I hope so,' she said, hoping she sounded amused.

'But I always walk down to the beach in the morning.' And because it was important to make sure he realised she hadn't followed him, she added, 'I didn't know you were swimming.'

He draped the towel around his taut waist and came towards her, big and male and overwhelming. 'Do you swim?'

'Every day.' She turned to go back to the house.

He fell in beside her. 'Not afraid of sharks?'

'Tiger sharks—the ones to be scared of—don't come into the lagoon much, if at all,' she told him, glad to be able to change the subject. 'And they're usually night feeders, so daylight swimming is pretty safe. Besides, the islanders say they're protected from them.'

He was too close. She felt an odd suffocation as they walked along the white shell path beneath the palms, and increased her pace.

Shortening his long stride to match hers, he asked, 'How are the islanders protected?'

So she told him the ancient story of the son of the first chief of the island who saved a small tiger shark—son of the chief of the sharks in the ocean around Rotumea—from a fish trap. 'For his compassion, the chief of all the sharks gave the islanders the right to be free of attack for ever. But only in the waters around Rotumea.'

He said, 'A charming story.'

Mischief glimmering in her smile, Jo looked up and said demurely, 'In all recorded history there's no account of any Rotumean being attacked by a tiger shark.'

His answering smile set off alarm bells all through her. *Stop it this moment*, she told her unruly emotions, tearing her gaze away to frown at the path ahead.

But that smile was a killer…

Hastily she said, 'I've left the makings for breakfast out, but if you want any more than cereal and fruit you'll have to get it for yourself. I have an appointment with Tom's solicitor at the resort at nine.'

And glanced up at his features for any hint that he knew of this.

Of course there was no alteration in the hard male contours of his face, and his eyes were hooded and unreadable. 'We'll talk when you've come back.'

Talk? About what?

The loan, she thought sickly.

Luc said, 'And I can get my own breakfast. I don't need looking after.'

An equivocal note in his voice kept her silent. She glanced at her watch. 'I don't imagine this meeting will last long. I assume it's to tell me what Tom wanted done with the house, so I'll go straight on to the shop afterwards.'

And spend the rest of the day trying yet again to work out how she could pay back that loan and still retain ownership of her fledgling business—an exercise she knew to be futile, as she'd already tried everything she could think of.

Think positively, she adjured herself robustly. Tom was too much of a realist not to know that his health was—well, not precarious, but the stroke had been a definite warning.

Surely if he felt anything at all for her beyond a mild affection for his housekeeper's niece he'd have made a fair provision for repaying the loan?

Bruce Keller looked up as Joanna Forman came into the room. Although he prided himself on his professional attitude, it took quite an effort to hide his curiosity.

He glanced at the documents on the table that served him as a desk. Joanna Forman, aged twenty-three, a New Zealand citizen, was not exactly how he'd imagined her. Tall, she had an excellent figure—she wasn't stick-thin like so many girls nowadays. And she had that intangible thing his daughters called style.

He wouldn't call her beautiful, yet as a man he could appreciate the subtle attraction of hair the colour of toffee and exquisite skin that seemed to radiate a softly golden glow. Not at all flamboyant—in fact, she should have looked out of place in the full-on exuberance of the tropics. That she didn't was probably due to her direct green gaze and softly sensuous mouth.

Yes, I see, he thought, and got to his feet, holding out his hand. 'Ms Forman?'

'Yes, I'm Jo Forman.' Her voice was steady, its slight huskiness adding to the impact of her mouth and her slender, curvy body.

He introduced himself, mentally approved the firmness of her handshake and said, 'Do sit down, Ms Forman. You do know why you're here?'

'You have something to tell me about Tom— Mr Henderson's—affairs. I presume it's that I need to vacate the house and pay back the loan he made me.'

Bruce blinked. She wasn't in the least what he'd imagined, and he needed to marshal his thoughts.

Tom Henderson had ignored his old friend's shocked cautions and flatly refused to discuss the arrangements he'd made for his mistress in his will, beyond making sure they were watertight.

The solicitor felt a twinge of professional pride at just how watertight they were.

No one would be able to break the terms of that will, not even Luc MacAllister—who'd almost certainly put a team of high-powered lawyers onto it once he'd learned what was in it.

After a slight cough Bruce said, 'No, there's nothing like that in his will.'

Surely she had some idea of the provision Tom had made for her?

She frowned, then seemed to relax a little. 'In that case, why am I here?'

Perhaps not...

Well, he'd soon see how that mouth looked when it smiled. He said, 'You're here because in his will Mr Henderson left you shares in his business enterprises worth several million New Zealand dollars.'

To his astonishment the soft colour fled her skin and she looked as though she might faint. No, he thought, wondering if he should offer a glass of water, modern young women didn't faint; that went out with the Victorians.

But after several moments of staring at him as though he'd grown horns, she regained her composure. *'What did you say?'* Her voice was low and intense, almost shaky.

Clearly she'd had no idea. The solicitor leaned

forward and told her the amount of money Tom Henderson had left her, finishing with, 'However, there are conditions to be fulfilled before the inheritance becomes yours.'

The muscles in her throat moved as she swallowed. Huskily she asked, 'Why?'

He started to tell her why Tom had made the conditions, but before he'd got far she cut him short. 'Why did he leave me *anything*?'

Startled, he felt his skin heat. 'I…ah, it seems that he felt—' He stopped, cleared his throat and resumed, 'That is, his affection for you made him want to…to make sure you were cared for.'

She frowned. 'Why?'

Her response showed a brutal understanding of her position. Clearly she was no romantic, and under no illusions as to her place in Tom Henderson's life. It was true very few men left their mistresses a fortune—even though in Tom's eyes this had been only a small fortune— so she should be elated.

Instead, she seemed aggressively astonished, if those two emotions were compatible.

Feeling his way, he asked, 'Does his reason matter?'

'Yes,' she told him unevenly. 'I think it does matter. He never said anything about this to me.'

Once more he cleared his throat and tried to

steer the meeting back on track. 'I don't know his reasons, I'm afraid. And as I said, there are conditions to this legacy.'

Breathless and dazed, Jo felt as though she'd been snatched from ordinary life and transported to an alternate universe. It took all of her energy to say, 'All right, tell me about them.'

And listened with mounting bewilderment and shock while he obeyed. He was careful to explain the legal jargon to her but, even so, it was too much to take in.

She took a ragged breath. 'Let me get this straight. You're saying that to inherit this…this money…I have to spend the next six months living with Luc MacAllister. Here, in Rotumea.'

And waited, almost holding her breath and hoping she'd got it terribly wrong.

The elderly solicitor nodded. 'That is so.'

Colour flooded her skin. Sitting upright, she said fiercely, 'Surely it must be illegal to make such conditions.'

'I thought I'd made it clear that Mr Henderson intended only that you occupy the same house,' the solicitor pointed out, not unsympathetically. He gave a little cough. 'Nothing more was intended than that.'

Fragments of thought chased each other fruitlessly through Jo's brain. She grabbed at one of them and blurted, 'I don't understand it. Why make such an imposition on me—on Mr MacAllister?'

'Mr Henderson didn't tell me, I'm afraid, but I imagine it was to safeguard you.' He paused, then added, 'It is a lot of money, Ms Forman, a lot of responsibility—' *more than you've been accustomed to*, his tone implied '—and there will be pitfalls. Mr MacAllister can help you manage this unexpected windfall and make sure you're aware of things that could go wrong.'

He'd sooner see me in hell, she thought trenchantly. Of course she'd need professional help to deal with so much money, but what had made Tom think his stepson would take on such a responsibility? Was this outrageous proviso some sort of revenge on Luc for ousting Tom from Henderson Holdings—and so successfully expanding it?

No, vengefulness didn't square with her knowledge of Tom. A sudden thought struck her. 'I don't have to accept this...the legacy, do I?'

After a shocked look, the solicitor said, 'Think about it carefully, Ms Forman. Mr Henderson wanted you to have this inheritance. His reasons for putting in such a condition are unknown, but it was important to him. He insisted on it being there, and he certainly felt it would be best for you.'

'That might be so but it's a complete imposition on L—Mr MacAllister.' Jo shivered, feeling the jaws of a trap close around her. She resisted the urge to wring her hands, and said bleakly, 'I can't believe Tom did this—or that Luc will accept such a charge.'

'He has already accepted it.'

Confused, she asked, 'He *knows* of this?'

'Yes.'

Well, of course he did. No wonder he'd believed Sean's assertion! He probably thought she'd weaselled her way into Tom's life in the hope of getting money, and now he was lumped with her for the next six months.

Her chin came up but, before she could speak, the elderly man on the other side of the table said gently, 'If you refuse Mr Henderson's legacy, your debt to his estate will have to be paid. And as he knew there will be occasions when you need money for various things, he set up an account for you with a monthly increment. But it cannot be used to pay off the loan.'

Her stomach clamped in a twist of pain. 'I don't want it,' she said automatically.

'Nevertheless, it is there.'

If Tom had wanted to help her from beyond the grave, why hadn't he just forgiven her the debt? What had been in his mind...?

Stop asking why, she ordered, because now she'd never know. *Concentrate on the facts.*

If she turned Tom's legacy down she wouldn't be the only person to suffer. So would the people who grew the ingredients for her lotions and creams on their small plantations, who relied on her business to pay for their children's education and medical care.

She could sell the fledgling business and pay off the debt. There had been tentative offers from a couple of big skincare firms who'd wanted to get their hands on a reliable source of several of the plants she used…

Even as the thought came into her mind she rejected it. When she'd first started using the islanders' recipes and plants for her skin products she'd promised the chiefs that if it became a success the business would stay in her hands.

She couldn't sell out and turn her back on them.

Her deep breath hurt her lungs. When she could speak again she said harshly, 'All right, I accept.'

And felt a clutch of fear at the prospect of what lay ahead.

Bluntly she asked, 'But what if Mr MacAllister changes his mind and refuses?'

There was a moment's silence. 'Then he loses

something that means more to him than money.'
And when she opened her mouth to ask him
what, he held up a hand. 'I can't reveal to you
what that is. But be assured, he will not refuse.'

CHAPTER FOUR

SAFELY PARKED BEHIND the shop, Jo switched off the Land Rover engine and sat with her hands gripped together in her lap, trying to stop shaking.

It had taken all her powers of concentration to negotiate the road between the resort and the town. Now her eyes stung with sudden tears, and she had to fight off a catch in her chest that threatened to turn into sobs.

Why had Tom left her such an enormous amount of money and burdened her with this weird condition? Why force her to live with Luc MacAllister for six months?

Biting her lip, she scrabbled in her bag for her handkerchief and wiped her eyes, dragging in a long shuddering breath.

Stop feeling betrayed, she told herself trenchantly, and work things out sensibly.

Tom knew she was intelligent and a quick learner, but he had a practical man's contempt for her degree. And of course it would be no help in dealing with that sort of fortune. She'd learned a lot from him, but the solicitor was probably right on the mark when he'd suggested Tom saw her as too young and inexperienced to be able to cope, so he'd made sure she couldn't do anything foolish with the legacy.

But *why* insist she spend the next six months with Luc MacAllister? Even before they'd met, Tom's unexpected legacy must have made Luc very ready to believe the worst of her. Sean's malice had only cemented that conviction in place.

The prospect of living with a man who thought she was little better than a tramp sent chills down her backbone.

Oh, Tom, she thought wretchedly, what were you thinking?

The car door swung open, and Savisi Torrens, the shop manager, leaned down to demand, 'Jo, are you all right? What's the matter?'

'I'm fine,' she said automatically, grabbing her bag.

Savisi scanned her face. 'You look pale. Are you sick?'

'No, no, I'm all right. Sorry, I was just thinking about things.'

'Have you had lunch?'

Surprised, Jo glanced at her watch. 'Not yet. I didn't realise it was so late.' She'd spent well over two hours with the solicitor. 'I'll get something from the café over the road.'

'Let me order that, and you can sit down while it's coming.' Savisi urged her into the relative coolness of the shop.

After she'd eaten a sandwich and drunk some coffee Jo felt better, although her stomach was still churning. It was a relief to discuss the monthly returns.

'The recession's hit us quite hard,' Savisi said succinctly. 'Not so many tourists this year.'

Jo scanned the figures again. 'Actually, we're doing better than I thought we might. Well done.'

The older woman disclaimed the praise. 'A good product always sells well.'

Jo said, 'I've been thinking that we might be able to set up some sort of sales outlet at the resort. Or a spa…'

'A spa? Oh, yes!'

Jo said quickly, 'It would cost a lot, but we might be able to swing it.' Even though Tom's legacy wouldn't be hers for six months…

'Meru's sister works at the resort—she might be able to tell you if the management would consider it.'

'I'd planned to see what she thinks.' Jo glanced

at her watch. 'I'm due at the factory in half an hour. But another thing I'm pondering is the packaging.' She mentally grimaced at the memory of Luc MacAllister's insultingly casual comment. 'Changing it would cost plenty too, but if we do go into the resort we'll need something more sophisticated.'

They discussed ideas over more coffee before Jo left to visit the small building where her range was manufactured.

Meru Manamai bustled out to greet her with her usual hug. Her reaction to Jo's idea was the same as Savisi's—and even more enthusiastic. 'I'll see what my sister thinks,' she said, 'but a spa sounds like a really good idea. I wonder why it wasn't part of the original plan?'

'Tom wasn't a spa person—he liked swimming in the sea.' Words wouldn't come until Jo pushed the sad memories away. 'Some of our skincare products would be useful there, but I'd need to develop others—massage oils, that sort of thing. I know mothers here massage their babies with coconut oil, so that would be a logical base.'

At Meru's nod she warmed to her theme. 'And if there's enough interest from the guests we could organise small tours of the factory. We could perhaps give free samples?' She grinned.

'Small ones, just enough to make a difference so they'd come back for more.'

Meru laughed, but said practically, 'It might work—people love to get something for free.' She gave Jo an anxious look. 'But a spa would cost a lot of money so perhaps now is not the time to consider it…'

But in six months' time Jo would have a lot of money… Everything seemed to be pushing her into accepting Tom's legacy.

'It would be really good for Rotumea,' she said thoughtfully. 'We'd probably have to import people who know different sorts of massage, but the Rotumean way of massaging would be a point of difference. Before we make any decisions I'll have to talk it over with the resort management.'

A spa would certainly get her product known internationally, and Luc's query about taking her line to the world tantalised her. Expansion would mean more jobs in Rotumea, the exhilaration of working to grow her business…

And huge risks, she reminded herself gloomily.

Later, driving home in the rapidly falling dusk, she braced herself to overcome her wary apprehension. Luc had every reason to profoundly dislike the position he'd been forced into.

At the house she switched off the engine and sat for a moment trying to ignore the tension knotting her stomach. She wouldn't—couldn't afford to—let herself get worked up about the situation, so when she discussed Tom's crazy scheme with Luc she'd be reasonable and tactful and practical. She would not, not, *not* allow her mind to be scrambled by the memory of the minutes she'd spent in Luc's arms, and the sensual impact of his kisses.

An impact she still felt, keen and precise like a dagger through armour, so that her blood throbbed thickly through her veins and she had to take several deep breaths before she could persuade herself to climb out of the vehicle and walk briskly into the house.

Only to realise that Luc wasn't there. Trying not to feel that she'd been given a reprieve, she set about preparing the dinner she'd bought at the market. Tom had always enjoyed the coconut and lime risotto cakes she made to go with fish, so fresh it still smelt of the sea, that she'd bought from a fisherman on her way home. It should please anyone but a certified carnivore who demanded red meat.

If that was Luc, tough.

She'd just put the mixture for the cakes into the fridge when instinct whipped her head around to meet a steel-grey gaze, hard as glacier ice and every bit as cold.

'Oh,' she said involuntarily. Her heart jerked violently, then seemed to skid to a stop for a second. She pulled herself together enough to say, 'I didn't hear you come in.'

'So I gather.' His tone was completely neutral, but she caught the darkness of contempt in his eyes, the same contempt she'd noticed when he'd held her and asked her what she wanted.

Still watching her, he leaned a hip against the counter that separated the kitchen from the rest of the house. Spooked by that unnerving survey, she said pleasantly, 'I usually have dinner in about half an hour's time. Is that all right for you?' And turned away.

'It's fine.' He glanced at his watch. 'Do you mind leaving the room? I need to talk to someone back home.'

'Of course. I'll go outside.' The telephone was an old handset, placed where any conversation could be heard right through the house.

Tom had rarely used it, so its position had caused no problems. Jo walked across the garden to pick a couple of Tahitian limes from the tree. Warned by the distant sound of Luc's voice that he was still talking, she stopped to haul out a seedling palm that had somehow managed to hide itself under a hibiscus bush. Tom had disdained tidy, formal gardens; this one was lush and thriving, its predominant greenness set off by brilliant blooms and exotic leaf forms.

She couldn't hear what Luc was saying, but the tone of his voice made it abundantly clear that he wasn't pleased. Not that he shouted; if anything his voice dropped, but the cold, unyielding menace in his tone raised bumps on her skin. He would, she thought with an inward shiver, make a very nasty enemy. So far he'd been reasonably polite to her; now she wondered why.

Silence from the house brought her upright. She picked up the limes, still warm from the sun, and walked inside, bracing herself for the discussion she knew they had to have.

Luc stood at the bar, his back to her as he poured drinks. Her steps faltering, she noted the strong lines of shoulders and back that tapered to lean hips above long, powerful legs. It didn't seem fair that one man should have so much—physical chemistry, a brilliant mind and that potent male charisma, as compelling as it was disturbing.

And extremely good hearing. Without turning, he said, 'I've finished. Come on in.'

She put the limes down on the table and stared

at the tall-stemmed glasses with the faint lines of bubbles rising through the pale liquid.

'Champagne?' she said uncertainly. 'What's the celebration?'

Eyes hooded, he handed her a chilled glass. 'I thought it appropriate,' he said with smooth arrogance. 'After all, you've just become a rich woman. Congratulations on a game skilfully played.'

Jo's fingers tightened around the slender stem so fiercely she thought she might snap it. OK, he was furious. She'd expected that, and she would not allow him to get to her.

Remembering her decision on the drive back, she thought *sensible, reasonable, practical...*

Trying to keep her voice steady, she said, 'I had no idea what Tom was going to do. I'm just as bewildered as you, and just as upset. I don't like being manipulated.'

His lip curled. 'Presumably he wanted to recompense you for your services. I only hope they were worth the money.'

Jo realised her teeth were clenched. If he was trying to goad her into losing her temper he was making an excellent job of it. Deliberately relaxing every taut muscle, she said, 'I don't blame you for being angry—Tom had no right to lumber you with my presence for the next six months. But if you think I'll be a whipping boy for your temper, think again. I'll walk out sooner than put up with insults.'

His face was unreadable, but his shrug conveyed much, and she had to stop herself from moving uncomfortably under his searching survey. 'I'm sure you won't,' he said, each word an exercise in contempt. 'Tom knew you'd stay.'

Goaded into indiscreet anger, she challenged, 'What about you? How did he make sure you'd fall in with his wishes?'

His smile was a taunt. 'Blackmail.'

Jo felt a momentary flare of sympathy, one that died when she met a gaze as harsh as a winter storm. Forcing a brisk, practical tone, she asked, 'So what happens now?'

'We leave for New Zealand tomorrow morning.'

Her jaw dropped. Recovering, she expostulated, 'I can't do that.'

'Why?'

'Because I'm needed here. I have responsibilities on the island—'

'Your little business?' he said, his negligent tone more galling than contempt would have been. 'You can keep an eye on it from New Zealand while we're away. But as you don't need it to pique Tom's interest any more it would be better to sell it.'

'I am *not* going to sell it,' she snapped, fighting back a rising tide of anger.

'Whatever. But you're coming to New Zealand tomorrow with me.' He examined her light, floating dress and drawled, 'You'll need warmer clothes, I imagine. I'll organise that.'

Her brows shot up. 'You're accustomed to buying clothes for women?'

With a smoothness that somehow grated, he said, 'My PA has excellent taste, and an encyclopaedic knowledge of the best places to hunt down the biggest bargains.'

His comment reminded her of the pathetic state of her bank balance. The small wage she took from her business barely covered her expenses in Rotumea. In New Zealand it would go nowhere. A hint of panic slowed her thoughts. No way could she afford new clothes. Second-hand shops?

She stifled a quiver of nervous amusement at the thought of Luc's PA seeking bargains for her in opportunity shops. Fortunately she had the perfect excuse. 'I can't afford any new clothes,' she said baldly.

In a voice that made her stiffen, Luc demanded, 'Use the money Tom left you.'

'I don't want it.' When he went to speak she added crisply, 'Living in Rotumea is cheap. I can manage on what I make.'

'You'll be spending some time travelling with me.'

Jo unclenched her teeth far enough to retort frigidly, 'Why? Tom knows—knew—how much the business means to me. I can't believe that he'd stipulate that I abandon it to jaunt around with you.'

Luc laughed, a cold, almost mocking sound. 'Welcome to the world of big money, Joanna Forman.' He raised his glass. 'The part of the will that dealt with my inheritance stated that when I go to any place that might help you, I am to take you with me.'

'Help me—in what way?'

'With your business, of course.' He sounded almost amused. 'Tom enjoyed power, and he probably relished the thought of forcing both of us to do his bidding from beyond the grave. So here's to his memory.' Luc drank some champagne, then set the flute down on the table with a sharp click.

Stung at this injustice, she said, 'Tom wasn't like that.'

'Then why did he do it?' he demanded, his tone derisory.

The same question she'd been asking herself since the solicitor had told her of the inheritance. The months ahead stretched out like a particularly testing purgatory.

Be reasonable, she told herself sternly, and forced herself to meet Luc's daunting gaze. 'I have no more idea than you do, but Tom would have had a reason. He wasn't an impulsive man. And we can't ask him, so it's useless speculating. I dislike the situation as much as you do, but the simplest way to deal with it is to take it one day at a time and try not to get in each other's way.'

'Indeed,' he said, a note of irony hardening the word. 'Unfortunately we have to share our lives for the next six months. That means there's no way of avoiding each other.' He paused, then added satirically, 'Unless you refuse the inheritance.'

And waited.

At that moment nothing—absolutely *nothing*—would have given Jo greater pleasure than to tell him fluently and with passion what he and that solicitor could do with Tom's bequest, and then turn and walk away.

Unfortunately she couldn't.

Before she was able to say anything Luc said

with hateful sarcasm, 'But you're not going to do that, are you?'

She stiffened her spine and met his sardonic look with every bit of resolution she possessed. 'No,' she said shortly. 'I owe Tom's estate money and the only way I can be sure of paying it off is to obey the terms of his will.'

'Selling the business would probably clear the debt.'

Jo masked her rising panic with a fierce look. 'When I started, I promised the local people I'd never sell it to an outsider. It's their knowledge I'm using, and they have an emotional stake in the business.'

'That's very noble of you.'

'What about you?' Her tone changed from defiance to challenge. 'What have you done that Tom was able to blackmail you into agreeing to stay here?'

'That,' he returned, his tone warning her she'd overstepped some invisible boundary, 'is none of your business.'

She shrugged. 'The reason I'm not walking away is none of your business either, but I told you anyway,' she said, then took a deep breath.

Remember—calm, reasonable, common sense, she reminded herself hastily.

Steadying her voice, she tried. 'Can't we just

agree to disagree and leave it at that? I don't like quarrelling, and the prospect of spending the next six months at loggerheads is not a pleasant one.'

A thought of amazing simplicity flashed across her mind like lightning. Without giving herself time to think, she asked, 'Why don't you take over Tom's loan to the business? Then I could pay it back under the same terms as I was paying Tom, and we'd not be forced to live together for six months.'

He was silent for a few seconds, and when his answer came it was brief and completely decisive. 'No.'

'That way I don't get Tom's inheritance which is causing you so much angst, and we don't have to put up with each other,' she pressed.

His brows drew together. 'No,' he said again. 'Tom wanted you to have the money. I'm not going to take it from you.'

Startled, she asked, 'Then why not accept the situation and try to make it as painless as possible? Would that be so difficult?'

Her plea met with no answer. She surveyed his face, lean and arrogant and unreadable, steely eyes half-shielded by his thick lashes. An uncomfortable silence stretched between them, taut and somehow expectant, thickening until Jo was desperate to break it.

She said, 'OK, I tried,' and turned away, only to stop abruptly when he spoke.

'Are you suggesting taking a different tack?' he asked without expression.

She looked over her shoulder. Something about his stance—alert, like that of a hunter—summoned a stealthy excitement that pulsed through her, fogging her brain.

'Exactly,' she flashed, feeling like prey.

'I must be losing my grip.' His voice was thoughtful, his gaze level. 'I'm not usually so obtuse.'

They seemed to be conducting two different conversations. She said uncertainly, 'I don't understand you.'

'I think you do. You should have couched your proposition in less obscure terms,' he said, reaching out to touch the nape of her neck.

Too late, Jo realised what he meant. She opened her mouth to tell him she'd made no proposition at all, but his touch sent shock scudding down her spine, a secret craving that smoked through her like some addictive drug.

'No!' she said, her voice dragging.

'Why not?'

He didn't sound angry. In fact, if she could

only trigger her brain into rational thought she'd guess his main emotion was amusement. The tips of his fingers were stroking softly, unexpectedly gentle, sending voluptuous, agitated shivers through her.

'Why not, Joanna?' he repeated, his voice cool, his gaze speculative.

She wasn't going to tell him that her experience was as limited as his kindness. Forcing herself to meet the intense blue flames that had banished all the grey from his eyes, she said hoarsely, 'Because, regardless of what you think, I'm not into casual sex.'

'One thing I can promise you,' he said, his tone suddenly raw, 'is that there would be nothing casual about it.'

And he pulled her into his arms.

Nothing—*nothing*—Jo had experienced had affected her like Luc's mouth on hers, the wildfire thunder of her pulse as his arms tightened to hold her against his lean body.

Before she had a chance to resist, sensation raced through her, his kiss detonating an involuntary response hot as fire, sweet as honey, fierce as the pressure of Luc's mouth on hers. When her knees buckled his arms tightened around her and her heart rate surged; he too was aroused.

Within Jo a pulse leapt into life, primal and dangerous, summoning a swift, mind-sapping hunger. As though aware of her vulnerability, Luc deepened the kiss, causing her body to flame into a passionate need that built on her response to his first kiss.

And then he lifted his head, breathed something short and brutal and let his arms fall, stepping back. For a moment her only emotion was heated resentment at his abrupt transition from passion to control. Fortunately common sense stiffened her spine and cleared her brain. She grabbed the back of a chair and dragged air into her lungs, her eyes wide and defiant as she forced herself to meet his hooded gaze. Disconnected fragments of thought tumbled through her brain. His face was drawn and fierce—a warrior's face—and the sensuous line of his mouth had tightened into hardness.

'I'm sorry,' he said curtly.

Jo's heart beat so loudly in her ears she couldn't hear the dull roar of the waves on the reef. She shook her head, finding that somehow her hair had escaped from its confining ponytail.

Surely Luc hadn't run his fingers through it…? The thought fanned an insidious tremor of something far too close to pleasure, reawakening her nervous turmoil.

He broke into her thoughts with a harsh order. 'Say something.'

'For once,' she retorted thinly, 'I'm speechless.'

Anger rode her, fuelled by shame. Once again she'd been entirely under the spell of his kiss. She despised herself because the embers of that desperate sensuality still smouldered deep inside her.

But his kiss had been an arrogant act of power—one reinforced by her mindless response. He'd no right to assume she was proposing some sort of grubby liaison, then kiss her like that.

Why hadn't she remained quiescent—detached and unimpressed—instead of going up like dry tinder in his arms?

Because she'd had no defence against the hypnotic masculinity of it, the sheer male hunger that had summoned a similar sexual drive from some unawakened place in her.

'I find that difficult to believe,' he said ironically. 'And to refer to what I said before we kissed, there was nothing light or casual about it.'

He paused, and when she said nothing he added, 'But you knew there wouldn't be. We've been far too conscious of each other ever since your eyes clashed with mine at the resort. Are you going to deny that?'

Jo drew in another sharp breath and evaded the question. 'That has nothing to do with anything.'

His smile was tinged with cynicism. 'It has everything to do with it. I wanted you then.'

Another blazing pang of desire shot through her. She resisted it, obstinately folding her lips before any foolish remark could escape.

Luc's expression remained unreadable. 'And your kisses tell me that you want me. Like you, I dislike the idea of spending the next six months quarrelling, so I'm suggesting a much more pleasant way of passing the time.'

He almost made it sound reasonable.

In his world, it probably was. Luc had probably made love to any woman he wanted.

Humiliated, Jo fought a treacherous urge to give in to this potent desire and walk on the wild side, explore a world she'd never experienced.

Fortunately, another, much more protective instinct blared a warning. Allowing herself to be persuaded, surrendering to his terms and becoming Luc MacAllister's lover would be a risk too unnervingly dangerous to take.

She would never be the same again.

So, although she had to force the words through

lips still throbbing from his kisses, she said stiffly, 'No. That's not what I want...'

His look—speculative and unsparing—shattered her already cracked composure, but she lifted her chin and continued, 'And when I suggested finding a way to spend the next six months other than quarrelling, I was *not* suggesting some sort of affair—if that's what you thought.'

Calmly he replied, 'In that case there's nothing more to be said. I apologise for misreading the situation. It won't happen again. Deal?' And he held out his hand.

Still dazed by her shocking need, she hesitated, then held out her own, shivering at the sensuous excitement that thrilled through her at his touch.

'Deal,' she said hoarsely, and forced herself not to snatch her hand away.

Six months...!

She winced, and broke into speech. 'Why do we have to leave tomorrow? It's going to make things difficult—not so much for me as for my manager.'

Luc frowned. 'I have to be in Auckland by tomorrow afternoon for a meeting.'

Something had obviously gone wrong, and Luc was going to deal with it.

But although he might be arrogantly accustomed to people accommodating themselves to his plans, she wasn't.

She said, 'That's impossible unless your meeting is very late in the afternoon. The next plane for New Zealand doesn't leave until two tomorrow afternoon.'

'A private jet will pick us up at eight tomorrow morning.' With an ironic smile he watched her eyes widen, and added, 'Also, I've just been informed that the following night Tom's favourite charity is holding a dinner in Auckland as a memorial to him.'

'So?'

'Apparently he wanted you to be there,' he said curtly. 'The charity is a children's hospital, and this is to raise funds for new equipment.'

Jo could think of nothing worse than going to such a dinner with him. One day at a time, she reminded herself with grim resignation, and surrendered.

'All right, but I can't just leave everything. I need to organise things—my shop and the factory, as well as someone to look after the house.'

'You've still got time,' he told her crisply. 'Time you're wasting in argument. Anyway, it's only going to be for a few days.'

Her lush mouth—its contours slightly enhanced by his kiss—tightened. Luc's body alerted him in an involuntary and infuriating response, heat twisting his gut as raw hunger ricocheted through him.

She said coldly, 'You could have told me that at the beginning.'

'I don't remember getting a chance,' he said sardonically. But she had a point. He took another sip of champagne, and asked, 'Is it so impossible?'

She stared at him for a moment, her green eyes shadowed. 'No,' she admitted quietly. 'But it's not just me it's going to inconvenience. If this sort of thing happens again I'll need more time to organise.'

He said abruptly, 'It's extremely important for me to be there—I'd have told you before but it's just come up.'

'The phone call,' she said, recalling with a remembered chill the tone of his voice.

'Yes,' he said shortly.

Clearly he had a very good reason for getting back to New Zealand as quickly as he could. However, if they were to spend the next six months together—as flatmates, she thought with a shiver—he was going to have to understand she wasn't some kid to be ordered around…

He waited until eventually she said, 'Very well, I'll be ready.'

For some reason his frown deepened. 'I'll organise a set-up for you so you can video conference with your managers whenever you want to.'

'Thank you.' She tried not to be swayed by his unexpected thoughtfulness. After all, he'd probably just order some minion to see that she had video contact.

Later, safely alone in her room, Jo collapsed onto the bed and tried to whip up some remnant of common sense. So Luc had kissed her. And she—reluctantly she admitted she'd almost *exploded* with what had to be lust.

Nothing she'd ever experienced had come near the sheer primal intensity of his kisses. She wasn't a virgin; in fact, she'd hoped her one serious relationship would lead to marriage. She'd loved Kyle, and been hurt when he made it clear that he resented her preoccupation with her mother's health. Her discovery a few weeks later that he was being unfaithful had shattered her.

Their lovemaking had been good, but nothing—*nothing* like being kissed by Luc.

That was a miracle of sensation—unbidden, reckless and clamorous, a torrent of response that too easily had drowned every sensible thought in barbaric hunger.

And it felt so *right*…as though it was meant to be.

Stifling a shocked groan, she looked around the bedroom and fought a cowardly urge to hurl her clothes into a bag and flee from an intolerable temptation.

Think, she adjured herself fiercely. *Use your head.*

For some reason Tom had believed it was important she spend six months in close—make that *very* close—contact with his stepson. And he'd made it pretty near impossible for her to turn his legacy down.

So she'd just have to grit her teeth and cope—without surrendering to this wild, irresponsible appetite she'd suddenly developed for Luc's body.

An ironic smile turned swiftly into a grimace. 'Oh, it should be so easy!' she muttered, pushing back the drift of netting that kept insects at bay.

Her sleep was restless, punctuated by dreams that faded as soon as she woke, leaving her aching and unsatisfied. In the morning she showered and dressed with care, then forced herself into the kitchen. One thing she was not going to do was walk out to the beach…

She was eating breakfast on the terrace when Luc appeared. 'Good morning,' she said sedately, refusing to respond to the sight of him in swimming trunks, drops of water polishing his sleek, tanned torso, his hair ruffled as though he'd merely run the towel over it.

His assessing look sent little ripples of excitement from nerve to nerve. 'Good morning. I won't be long—no, stay there. I can get my own breakfast when I've changed.'

And he disappeared into the bedroom.

Her heartbeat soared uncomfortably when he reappeared, dressed in a casual pair of trousers and a short-sleeved shirt. Chosen for him by whom? His mother? No, she'd died several years ago. A lover?

Someone who knew him very well, because the colour matched his eyes.

Without preamble, he said, 'We need to talk.'

Jo tried to match his pragmatic unemotional tone. 'When you've had your breakfast. Would you like some coffee?'

He gave her another of those straight looks. 'If you're having some yourself. You don't need to wait on me. I'm capable of making my own coffee. And my own meals.'

'It's habit,' she said calmly. 'I acted as Tom's hostess, so I do it automatically.'

Actually, she needed something bracing— a cold shower would be good—but coffee was supposed to make one more alert. Besides, it meant she could get herself out of his way without looking stupid.

It was all very well to spend half the night telling herself she could cope with the rush of sensual adrenalin that ambushed her every time she saw Luc, but when she actually laid eyes on him she had no defence against the hunger aching through her.

Getting to her feet, she said, 'Anyway, I need some and I might as well make some for you too.'

A false move, because he came with her into the kitchen and while she organised the coffee he assembled his breakfast.

She should have absented herself while he ate, she thought as she sat opposite him and drank her coffee. Sharing breakfast was altogether too intimate.

Mug in hand, she got to her feet and wandered across to the edge of the decking, keeping her gaze fixed on a bird with a yellow bandit's mask as it fossicked in the thick foliage of a hibiscus bush.

'What bird is that?' Luc's voice came from very close behind her.

She jumped, and whirled around. His hand

shot out and gripped her shoulder for a moment, before releasing her.

Her breath locked in her throat as she stared mutely at him.

What could have been triumph gleamed for a moment in his hard eyes.

No! Gathering all her strength, Jo forced herself to turn away, to fix her gaze on the bird, now warily checking them out from the fragile shelter of the leaves.

In a distant voice she said, 'It's a native starling.'

The bird shot out from behind its leafy screen, flying straight and true, its alarm call alerting every other bird to a threat. Previously Jo had always been a little amused at the starlings' propensity for drama and flight.

Now she knew exactly how they felt. Threatened.

Quickly she said, 'They're an endangered species. Tom and the chiefs were working on a way to save them. Unfortunately, that means killing off the doves that were introduced a century or so ago. They compete with the starlings for food and nesting sites. And the locals like the cooing of the doves. They call them the lullaby birds. Sadly for the starlings, they can only produce that harsh screech.'

She was babbling and it was almost a relief when Luc said from behind her, 'I'm sure Tom would have overcome that prejudice. He didn't like being beaten—and, as we both know, he had a ruthless streak a mile wide.'

Indeed. And it would be useless to keep asking herself what on earth Tom had intended to bring about with his condition.

Only one thing was certain; he'd have had a motive.

Actually there was another certainty—neither she nor the man with her would ever learn what that motive was. Unless Luc MacAllister already knew...

But he'd said he didn't, and she was inclined to believe him. Quickly, before she could change her mind, she turned and asked, 'Do you really have no idea why Tom would have done this?'

His already tough face hardened. 'No idea apart from the one I suggested yesterday—a determination to force both of us to his will.'

CHAPTER FIVE

Jo SHOOK HER head. 'I can't believe that,' she said decisively and with some heat.

Luc recalled her objection of the previous day. *Tom wasn't like that.*

Not with her, perhaps.

But he didn't say it aloud. For some reason it irritated the hell out of him to accept she'd been Tom's lover. More infuriating was the fact that she wanted him to believe she'd felt something more for his stepfather than the mercenary greed of her sort of woman.

But what really made him angry was the fact that her kisses had almost convinced him she'd been feeling genuine desire.

With hard-won cynicism—based on being a target too many times to recall—he'd been sure he could tell the real thing from the fake. Clearly she was good…

Well, Tom only went for the best.

Abruptly he asked, 'Have you packed?'

Her answer was even more curt. 'Yes.'

She sat silently on the way to the airfield, watching Luc talk to the taxi driver from the back of the car. The tropical sun warmed the cool olive of his skin, outlined the breadth of his shoulders and limned his arrogant profile with gold when he glanced sideways at the resort as they drove past.

So, he turned her on. *Get over it—and fast*, she ordered, and dragged her gaze away to stare blindly at the pink and yellow flowers of the frangipani bushes along the road.

Oh, face the truth! He did much more than turn her on; he set her alight, stirring her blood so she had to fight stupidly erotic thoughts. And the memory of his kiss sent hot, secret shudders right down to her toes.

She had to make some rules—unbreakable ones. The first was obvious. No more kissing—it was too dangerous. She'd liked it far too much.

Actually, she accepted reluctantly, *liked* didn't come near it. She couldn't come up with words that described what Luc's kisses did to her.

And she wasn't going to try. Dwelling on her weakness was not only stupid, it was reckless and forbidden.

The private jet was a revelation, and provided some distraction. She tried not to stare like some hick, but the opulent, ostentatious décor was blatantly designed to impress. Which surprised her; Luc didn't seem a man to indulge in such crass showmanship.

'You don't like it,' he said as she looked around.

She gave him a suspicious glance. 'I don't have to, do I?' she asked sweetly.

He smiled. 'It's not mine. I chartered it because it's fast and safe, not for the interior decoration. Buckle up; we're ready to go.'

She watched Rotumea fall away beneath them, a glowing green gem in a brilliant enamelled sea of darkest blue that faded swiftly to green. A mixture of emotions—part anticipation, part regret—ached through her heart.

Goodbye, Tom, she thought, before chiding herself for being overly dramatic.

'What's the matter?' Luc asked.

Startled, she looked up. 'Nothing,' she said quietly, wishing he weren't so perceptive.

After a disbelieving glance he handed her a magazine, a glossy filled with the latest in fashion. 'Is this all there is to read?' she enquired dulcetly.

'I believe it has excellent articles.' The amusement in his voice almost summoned a smile from her.

'Oh, that's all right, then.'

Whoever had told him that was right—it was both provocative and entertaining, as well as featuring the latest fashions.

Her incredulous gaze fell onto a photograph in the social pages. There stood Luc, elegantly dressed at some race meeting, and beside him a glamorous redhead.

His fiancée, according to the caption. Shocked into stillness, Jo blinked, forcing herself to keep her gaze on them, while something like cold rage squeezed her heart. How dare he kiss her when he was engaged?

A lean hand came over and flipped the magazine closed so she could see the publication date. A year and a half previously...

'Long out-of-date. Perhaps I could get a reduction in the charter fee,' Luc said. 'The week after that was taken she eloped with Tom's nephew. They're married now, with a baby on the way.'

'Oh,' Jo said inadequately, furious with herself because her first emotion was a violent relief, followed almost instantly by astonishment at the ironic amusement in his tone.

Clearly he hadn't grieved too long at the couple's betrayal.

She said, 'Tom's nephew? He didn't mention it.' Then wished she'd stayed silent.

'Possibly he didn't think you'd be interested,' he said negligently.

Or perhaps Tom hadn't considered it to be any of her business. He'd fleetingly referred once to a past relationship of Luc's with the daughter of an Italian billionaire, and she remembered a casual conversation about Luc's mother's hope he'd marry into the French aristocracy she'd come from.

Apart from that, nothing about Luc's personal life.

The seatbelt sign tinged off, and automatically she looked up. Luc met her gaze, his mouth curved into a satirical smile. 'I believe much the same thing happened to you,' he said coolly.

She went rigid. 'How did you know?'

'Don't look so startled.' He shrugged. 'When you moved in with Tom I had you checked out, of course.'

Outraged and a little afraid, she spluttered, 'You had a nerve!'

His gaze was keen and unreadable. 'As I said last night, welcome to the world of the rich and powerful. And your lover was a selfish pup to make you choose between your mother and him.'

'He didn't think—' She stopped again.

'Go on.'

It was her turn to shrug. Discovering that Kyle disliked her mother had been bad enough; what had shattered her was that he'd believed all the gossip about Ilona.

'He didn't like her,' she said stiffly.

'Why?'

Because he thought she'd been little better than a call girl. In their final argument before he'd left Jo he'd laughed in her face when she'd mentioned marriage, and told her brutally that no woman with a mother like Ilona Forman would be a suitable wife for him.

It still stung. Jo looked down at the magazine and turned the page, saying distantly, 'They just didn't get on.'

Luc nodded and bent to open a folder. After a few moments he realised that although he had a bitch of a meeting ahead of him, he couldn't concentrate.

Joanna's lover had probably realised her mother was being totally unreasonable to demand such devotion. She'd spent much of her daughter's childhood foisting her onto her sister while she flitted around the world on modelling shoots, walking the big catwalk events and being a muse to designers—whatever the hell a muse was.

At least she'd left her daughter enough money to start her business.

He had to admire Joanna for that. Even with Tom's help and advice, getting her skincare product out onto the marketplace, steering it into profit must have taken guts, creativity and hard work.

And loyalty to those who worked for her.

Not that he'd change his mind about her. And in six months' time she'd be amply recompensed for her services to Tom.

Warily Jo sent a surreptitious glance his way. He was frowning as he read his documents, black brows drawing together over that uncompromising blade of a nose. Jo looked quickly back at the magazine, glad she wasn't the person or persons waiting for him to arrive in Auckland.

Shortly afterwards the steward came into the cabin with an offer of morning tea. Luc drank his the same way he drank coffee—black and to the point. Jo liked hers with milk, and after finishing it and one of the small muffins that accompanied it, she sat back on a wide sofa while Luc went back to his folder.

In Auckland it was raining, a soft autumn shower that stopped before the steward slid the door open. Shivering a little in the cool air, Jo hurried inside to be processed by customs and immigration officers.

Luc said abruptly, 'I'll organise an immediate advance of the money Tom left you.'

'Were there any conditions?' she asked with a snap.

'Bruce Keller wouldn't tell me if there were,' he returned indifferently. 'If he didn't say anything to you, then no, there were no conditions.'

She sighed. 'Thanks. And I'm sorry I bit— I'm already tired of this situation.'

And tired of being forced down a road she'd not planned to take. It hurt to think that Tom had done this to her—hurt more that her image of him was slowly crumbling.

'Think of the end result.' It was impossible to discern Luc's emotions from his voice. 'Give Bruce Keller the data and he'll make sure the money is in your bank account.'

Jo bit her lip. 'You have his contact details?'

Luc's brows lifted. 'I do.'

Well, of course. Clearly he thought he was dealing with an idiot. Heat warmed her face. If he hadn't whisked her so unceremoniously off the island she'd have been better prepared.

But she didn't care a bit what Luc MacAllister thought of her.

'Where are we going?' she asked, looking around as they left the building.

'To Tom's place on the North Shore.'

The house on the North Shore was about as different as anything could be from Tom's home in Rotumea, although it nestled into a garden of palms and luxuriant foliage beside a beach on Auckland's magnificent harbour. Jo examined the double-storeyed building of classic, clean architectural lines and much glass as the car eased up the drive.

'Very tropical in feel,' she observed when the car drew up outside a double-height door.

Luc sent her a narrow glance, clearly recognising the jibe. 'Tom's natural environment,' he said calmly, switching off the engine in front of a huge double door. 'Auckland has a pretty good climate for outdoor living. I'm sure you made the most of it while you lived here.'

'Of course,' she said automatically, then stiffened. She couldn't recollect having told him she'd spent her childhood in Auckland.

Of course, he'd had her investigated—hired some sleazy private detective to poke around her life looking for dirt.

Distaste shivered through her, alleviated only by the cheering thought that it must have been a very boring investigation for whoever had done it.

Chin angled away from Luc, she got herself out of the car and went around to the boot where he'd stowed their cases. The soft sound of waves on the shore eased her tension a little, yet made her feel wrenchingly homesick for Rotumea.

One day at a time, she reiterated briskly, and reached in to get her pack from the boot.

Only to have Luc take it out. 'It's all right, I can manage,' she said stiffly.

'So can I.' After hauling his own suitcase free, he set off for the huge front door.

Baulked, she walked beside him, and was startled when the door was opened by a middle-aged man with an expressionless face.

He was Sanders, she was informed as Luc introduced them. Jo had never met a man with only one name before, and he seemed surprised when she held out her hand and said, 'How do you do.'

He shook it but dropped it as quickly as he could.

This was not at all like Rotumea, or the New Zealand she'd grown up in. Perhaps the two years she'd spent in the tropics had turned her into a yokel.

No, it was just that she'd become accustomed

to the Rotumean way of doing things. In such an isolated society, almost everyone could find some blood relationship—however distant—so there was little social distinction. And Tom had fitted in really well—although, she conceded as she walked sedately into a high, light-filled entrance hall, he had been allotted the status of high rank in Rotumea...

As Luc would be. There was something about him that indicated strength—and not just of body. He moved with the lithe athleticism that spelt perfect health. One look at his hard countenance was all it took to appreciate the honed intellect and forceful personality behind his autocratic features.

'Is there something wrong with my face?'

His ironic voice brought her back to herself. Oh, hell, she'd been staring...!

'Not that I can see,' she said flippantly, hoping he wouldn't notice the heat burning across her skin. She looked around the high, spacious hall and breathed, 'This is lovely.'

'It was Tom's design.'

Surprised, she said, 'He didn't tell me he was an architect.'

'He wasn't, but he had definite ideas, and he worked closely with the architect, a chap called Philip Angove.'

'I've heard of him—I read an article not long ago that called him the only real successor to Frank Lloyd Wright.'

'I suspect he wouldn't exactly be pleased at the comparison, but he's brilliant.' Luc laughed. 'He and Tom had some magnificent differences of opinion, but Tom felt the result was worth the effort. I'll show you to your room while Sanders organises lunch.'

Her room was large, with its own wide balcony overlooking a pool—yet clearer evidence of Tom's profound love for the tropics. More palms and a wide terrace surrounded the pool, and the gardens featured the same hibiscuses that grew wild in Rotumea, but instead of the island's tropical abandon this garden had a lush, disciplined beauty.

'The en suite is through there,' Luc said, nodding at a door in the wall. He glanced at his watch. 'Lunch will be in half an hour—I'll collect you. If you like, Sanders can unpack for you.'

'No, thanks,' she said hurriedly. Sanders might be accustomed to doing such chores, but she wasn't accustomed to having them done for her.

Luc's smile was tinged with irony. 'There's nothing of that slapdash tropical informality in

Sanders. He's British and has stern ideas about what is proper and what isn't. You'll get used to him,' he said. 'He, on the other hand, might find you bewildering.'

Childishly, she pulled a face at the door as it closed behind him, but quickly sobered, turning away to draw in a deep breath and set herself to unpacking. The wardrobe, she discovered, was a dressing room. She hung up the contents of her pack, smiling a little ruefully at the tiny amount of space her clothes took up.

But once showered and dressed in a shirt of clear blue over slender ivory trousers she walked across to the window and looked out beyond the pool. Beyond it, through the dark foliage of the pohutukawa trees that fringed all northern coastlines, she caught a glimpse of white sand and the sea.

Her main emotion, she realised with surprise, was a profound sense of homecoming.

Putting aside the fact that the man she was to share her life with for six months thought she was little better than a prostitute, it was good to be back.

So she'd just keep out of Luc's way.

A knock on the door set her pulses haywire, forcing her to admit that she'd grossly oversimplified her emotions. The kisses they'd shared, backed up by Luc's admission that he wanted her, meant she'd never feel completely at ease with him.

With a silent heartfelt vow that she wasn't going to lose her head over him, she squared her jaw and opened the door, only to feel her foolish heart sing at the sight of male temptation in a business suit that moulded itself lovingly to his powerful frame.

'Ready?' he asked.

'Yes.' OK, so she was going to have to work on controlling her body's disconcerting response. She'd do it. Familiarity had to breed contempt. As her mother used to say occasionally, very few men were worth a single tear. Absolutely.

Lunch was set out on the wide roofed terrace leading to the pool. Without thinking, Jo picked three frilly, silken hibiscus flowers and arranged them in a scarlet dazzle at one end of the table.

Looking up, she caught Luc's eyes on her and realised what she'd done. 'Sorry,' she said, ignoring an odd quiver somewhere in the pit of her stomach. 'Habit dies hard.'

'Feel free.' He clearly couldn't have been less interested.

It wasn't the first time she'd eaten with him, yet the tension she always felt in his presence had become supercharged with a heady awareness that set her on edge.

Unlike Luc, who seemed fully in control. Trying to match his cool reserve, she masked her inner turmoil, and they ate the meal like polite strangers.

She was relieved when he left for his very important meeting, but after a few irritating minutes spent wondering how he was dealing with whatever emergency he was involved in, she opened her elderly laptop and began to work on it.

The afternoon dragged. Sanders delivered her afternoon tea, followed by dinner without any sign of Luc.

Forget about him, she ordered, and applied herself even more rigidly to work.

A knock on her door near ten that night brought her head up from weary, frustrated contemplation of the screen. Heart jumping, she forced herself to walk sedately across the room and open the door.

'What's the matter?' Luc demanded after one penetrating glance.

'My computer's died,' she told him baldly.

He looked a little tired, his olive skin drawn more tightly over his autocratic features. Jo felt an odd impulse to tell him to go to bed and get a good night's sleep.

Fortunately it was derailed when he demanded, 'How much have you lost?'

'Nothing—it's all backed up—but it won't work, no matter what I do to it.' She would have liked to know how the important meeting had gone, but she didn't have the right to ask.

'Let me see it.'

Reluctantly she stood back to let him in. One grey glance took in the laptop set up on the makeshift desk, and he said, 'How old is that?'

'I don't know.'

'No wonder it died. It looks like a relic from the eighties.'

'Possibly it is,' she retorted with some asperity, 'but it's worked fine up until now.'

His stepfather wouldn't have been able to resist trying to find out the problem, but Luc said, 'You need a new one.'

'I know.' Jo didn't try to hide her frustration. Why did the wretched thing have to break down at the most inconvenient moment?

Luc gave her another of his penetrating looks. 'I'll lend you one of mine until you organise a new one.'

Surprised, she said, 'Won't you be needing it?'

'Not this one.' His incisive reply cut short her instinctive response to refuse.

Abruptly abandoning the computer, he went

on, 'I forgot to tell you to let Sanders know about any food you're allergic to or dislike hugely, and he'll make sure it doesn't appear on the menu.'

'He's already asked, thank you, before he cooked dinner. But Luc, I can make my own meals—'

He gave her a brief smile. 'Not in his kitchen you won't.'

'Oh. OK.'

Clearly she needed to know the boundaries of Sanders' sphere of influence, but before she could ask tactfully, Luc said, 'Is there anything you need or want now?'

'No, thanks.'

He nodded. 'The computer will be here tomorrow morning—probably after I leave for another meeting, one that might last all day.' Grey eyes scanned her face. 'Go to bed,' he commanded. 'You look exhausted.'

'Fury with an inanimate object can do that to you,' she said wearily. 'Goodnight.'

She slept heavily, so soundly she didn't wake until after nine. Sanders appeared as she came down the stairs, and said, 'Mr MacAllister has left. He thought you might like to eat breakfast on the terrace.'

'That would be lovely,' she said, and smiled at him. His response was a mere movement of his lips, but he seemed a little less stiff than previously. 'I'm sorry if I've interrupted your routine. I don't normally sleep in.'

He unbent enough to say, 'Travelling has that effect on some people.'

It seemed a shame to waste such a glorious, beckoning day indoors, but once she'd finished work she could spend time in the pool.

The computer arrived around ten, with a desk and an office chair as well as a set of shelves and a filing cabinet. Under Sanders' supervision they were carried into her room and a temporary office was set up.

It worked well; the computer had been cleared and once she'd had a little more practice at dealing with its foibles she'd be fully confident with it. She ate lunch out on the terrace, and was on her way back to her room when the telephone on a hall table rang. Automatically she picked it up and said, 'Hello.'

'Who is this?' a woman demanded. 'Have I the wrong number? Is this Luc MacAllister's house?'

'Yes.' Answering had not been such a good idea, especially when she looked up and saw Sanders—more poker-faced than normal—advancing towards her, intent on taking over.

'Are you a cleaner?' the woman asked. 'Where is Sanders?'

Chagrined, she said, 'Sorry. He's on his way,' handed over the receiver to him and escaped.

But not fast enough to avoid hearing Sanders say, 'Certainly, Ms Kidd. I'll make sure Mr MacAllister gets your message.'

Whoever she was, Ms Kidd had no manners. And Jo had to endure a mortifying moment when Sanders told her that answering the telephone was his duty.

'Yes, I realised that,' she said ruefully. 'I'm afraid it was an automatic reaction.'

He relaxed infinitesimally. 'Mr MacAllister has all his calls screened except on his personal phone. You'd be surprised the sort of people who try to get in touch with him—reporters and such.' His tone indicated that reporters and poisonous snakes had a lot in common.

'I won't do it again,' she told him.

He nodded and said, 'Mr MacAllister's personal assistant has just rung. She'll be here in half an hour to take you shopping.'

'What?' she said, bewildered, before remembering the conversation about clothes she'd had with Luc.

'For tonight's dinner, I understand,' Sanders elaborated.

She'd pushed any thought about the dinner out of her mind, but had to admit to a secret relief that Luc had remembered.

CHAPTER SIX

LUC'S PERSONAL ASSISTANT turned out to be a superbly dressed woman in the prime of her life. At first Jo guessed her to be in her forties, but after half an hour or so in her company, she changed her mind. Sarah Greirson was probably the best-preserved sixty-year-old she'd ever come across. With a mind like a steel trap, an infectious sense of humour and an encyclopaedic knowledge of Auckland's best bargains, she made shopping for the dinner gown an amusing and fascinating experience.

In turn, she was intrigued by Jo's fledgling business. So much so that when they returned to the house Jo raced up to her room and returned with a jar of rehydrating cream.

'Thanks for being so helpful,' she said, and gave it to her.

Sarah looked taken aback. 'Are you sure?' she asked.

'Sure of what?' Luc said, appearing unexpectedly in the huge sliding doors that led out onto the terrace.

Jo jumped, colour beating up through her skin. Very aware of the older woman's perceptive gaze on her, she said swiftly, 'Of course I'm sure. I'll be interested to see how you like it.'

'I'm *very* interested in trying it out,' Sarah said cheerfully. 'Thanks so much.' She turned to Luc. 'And thank you for asking me to do this. Once I'd convinced her that hiring a dress would not be a good look we had a great time, and she'll be stunning.'

'Of course,' Luc said smoothly. 'She always is. I've got some papers for you before you leave, Sarah.'

Alone, Jo let out a ragged breath, and closed her eyes before walking out onto the terrace.

She always is... What was he up to? She waited until her heart rate levelled out, only for it to shoot up again when she turned to see Luc standing in the doorway, watching her with a quizzical amusement that brought another flush to her cheeks.

'Tired?' he asked, walking across to her.

'No—at least, yes, a bit.' She produced a smile. 'Sarah is a perfectionist in every sense of the word. Standing around has never been my thing, especially when people are inspecting me as though I'm a piece of meat, and discussing my measurements to the last centimetre.'

His brows lifted. 'You're pleased with the result?'

'It's a beautiful dress. And so are the shoes and the bag.'

Not to mention the new bra Sarah had insisted on, and the sheerest of tights.

She finished, 'Sarah has superb taste, and fortunately we agreed. I won't shame Tom. And I'll pay you for them when I get access to the money Tom left me.'

His expression didn't alter, yet a tenuous shiver snaked the length of her spine. 'You won't,' he said curtly.

She stopped herself from biting her lip, but ploughed on, 'That's why he left it, so I wouldn't be an expense on you. And, speaking of expenses—we need to talk about sharing them.'

Frowning, he said, 'We do not.'

Jo opened her mouth to expostulate, but the words died unsaid when he reached out and put a finger across her lips. Eyes widening, she froze, her heart thudding uncomfortably in her ears. Every nerve tightened; she could see a pulse beating in his throat.

He was too close—suffocatingly close. Her brain wouldn't work and she couldn't move.

Very quietly, in a tone that meant business, he said, 'I don't need any contributions to household expenses.'

'And I don't need charity—' she began, then stopped, stomach knotting because each word felt like a kiss against his finger. She could even taste him—a smoky male flavour that spun through her like a whirlwind.

He dropped his hand and stepped back. 'It's not charity. I want something from you.'

She'd just drawn a swift breath, but his final sentence drove it from her starving lungs. 'What?'

Her voice was too fast, too harsh, but she thought she knew what he wanted, and his proposition was going to hurt both her pride and her heart.

'Not what you think,' he said curtly, each word cutting like a whiplash. 'I don't need to buy or blackmail women into my bed.'

He paused. Jo waited, conscious of a vast feeling of relief alloyed by a sneaky and wholly treacherous regret.

When he resumed it was in that infuriatingly ironic tone. 'You're making heavy weather of this, Joanna. It's only for six months—in the grand scheme of your life barely long enough to consider.' He added on a cynical note, 'And think of the reward when it's over and you can thumb your nose at whoever you want to.'

Stung, she retorted, 'Thumbing my nose is not my style.' Her smile showed too many teeth. 'In fact, I don't believe I've ever seen anyone do it. Have you?'

'What a deprived life you've led,' he remarked idly. 'Children do it all the time.'

'Not me. Did you?'

He grinned. 'Only once. My mother caught me and after her scolding I never did it again. She said it was vulgar, and although I was too young to understand what that meant I understood it was bad.'

Intrigued, she said, 'So you were a good kid and obeyed her.'

He raised his brows. 'Of course,' he said. 'Didn't you obey your mother?'

'Most of the time,' she said wryly. Her indulgent mother had made up for the times she'd been away with treats and much love. A little raw at the memories, she asked, 'So what do you want from me?'

'A truce.'

Her brows shot up. 'I believe I suggested that not so long ago.'

'You did, and I agree—the least disagreeable way of coping with the next six months is to ignore the fact that we're forced to obey Tom's whim, and get on with our respective lives without getting too much in each other's way.'

Of course he was right. She should be glad he'd seen reason—she *was* glad he'd seen reason and agreed with her. It was the sensible, practical, *safe* attitude.

Right now she needed safety very much.

So she nodded firmly. 'It's a deal,' she said and added rapidly, 'I've never been to a charity dinner. How do they run?'

'Drinks and mingling first, then excellent food, then a comedienne.' His smile held wry humour. 'I suspect the entertainer was chosen more for her looks than her wit.'

Some hours later, her hair coiled sedately at the back of her neck, Jo examined herself in the mirror. Wearing the clothes Luc had paid for, her make-up as perfect as she could get it, she thought dryly that she had one thing to thank heaven for—he hadn't held out his hand to seal the deal. She recalled only too vividly the way her intransigent body had responded to his touch.

As though champagne instead of blood coursed through her veins...

She was going to have to overcome this fascination, the way one look from those hard grey eyes sent chills—delicious, sparkly, *sexy* chills through every cell in her body.

'And you are just one out of a million or so women who probably suffer the same silly reaction whenever he looks at them,' she told her reflection, and turned—carefully—to pick up the evening bag Luc had also paid for.

She'd spent some time practising walking in the strappy shoes, but was still cautious. Two years spent in the tropics, where footwear was either sandals or thongs, hadn't prepared her for heels. She crossed her fingers against any chance of tripping.

Luc watched her come down the stairs, noting that Sarah had done a magnificent job. Critically he decided he preferred that sensual mass of amber hair loose, but the bun at the back of her neck certainly gave her an elegant, sophisticated air.

The ankle-length dress—a slim thing a shade darker than her hair—skimmed Joanna's curves. Too closely, he thought, his body tightening. He chided himself for being a fool; possessiveness had never been a problem in his previous relationships. He'd expected fidelity—

Where the hell had that thought come from?

They were not in a relationship, and weren't going to be.

He resumed his survey, noting the swift burn of colour along her cheekbones. A piece of jewellery set off her slender wrist, a metal cuff the same colour as the dress.

And she walked like a queen, head held high, straight-backed and slender.

She looked exactly the way he wanted—like his lover, dressed by him, ready for him.

However, the glance she gave him when she reached the bottom of the staircase was narrowed, her smoky green eyes direct and challenging. 'I hope you think this was worth it,' she said with a lift of her square chin.

'Every cent,' he said coolly, enjoying the sparring.

'Which I'll pay back as soon as I get Tom's money,' she reiterated firmly. 'And you should give Sarah a nice bonus. She deserves it.'

He took her arm, feeling her tense against him as he turned her towards the door. 'I don't discuss Sarah's salary.'

'I wasn't discussing her salary. I was subtly pointing out that I'm sure her job description doesn't include dressing your dinner partners.'

She smelt delicious, softly sensuous as a houri. To stop the swift clamorous surge from his body, he said, 'It includes whatever I want her to do. How are you getting on with the heels?'

'Warily. Ambling along the beach at Rotumea in bare feet is no training for heels this high.'

Her words summoned a vivid image—sleepy, golden and sleek as she rose from the hammock in her bikini, and again his body reacted with a fierce, primitive hunger. Controlling it was surprisingly difficult. 'Do you want me to walk you like this, or is it easier if you step out on your own?'

She relaxed a fraction. 'I hate to admit it,' she confessed, 'but it will probably be better for my confidence to lean on your arm.'

'In that case, use me as a prop whenever you want to.'

On the drive across the bridge he started to tell her about the charity, then broke off. 'I suppose you've already heard of this from Tom.'

'No,' she said. 'I knew he supported charities but he never spoke of them.'

'Possibly he thought you wouldn't be interested.'

'I'd say he realised I can't yet afford to support anything,' she said crisply. 'He wasn't the sort of man to boast about his generosity.'

He looked down at her, his teeth flashing

white in a humourless smile. 'I've never thought of Tom as being sensitive.'

'He did a lot of good for Rotumea and its people.'

'He could afford it, and he enjoyed his holidays there.'

Jo frowned at his dismissive tone. 'Didn't you like him?'

'He was a good stepfather,' he said evenly. 'Strict but very fair. He did his best for me, just as I'm sure he did his best for the islanders—for anyone who worked for him, in fact.'

He sounded as though he was discussing a schoolmaster, she thought and wondered again. Had the struggle for control after Tom's stroke soured their relationship too strongly for any repair?

At the venue they were ushered into a room filled with women in designer gowns and men in austere black and white. No one stared—or if they did, Jo thought, they made sure neither she nor Luc noticed. Yet she felt out of place and acutely self-conscious, especially when an exquisite woman swayed up to them, her smile a little set, her gaze softly shielded.

'Luc,' she breathed, and reached up to kiss him with all the aplomb of someone who knew she wouldn't be refused.

A fierce sense of denial ripped through Jo when Luc inclined his head so the woman's mouth grazed his cheek. She forced her stiff body to relax. Even that one syllable revealed who the woman was—the Ms Kidd of the phone call.

He straightened and said, 'Natasha, you haven't yet met Jo Forman, who's staying with me.'

He introduced them, adding, 'Natasha is the star of a very popular television show.' And with a smile at the other woman, he explained, 'Joanna has spent several years overseas, so she doesn't yet know anything about local television.'

What to say? Jo fell back on a platitude. 'Congratulations. I'll look forward to seeing it.'

In return, she got a practised smile and a look that was keenly suspicious. 'Thank you,' Natasha Kidd said sweetly. 'I hope you enjoy it.' She glanced up at Luc. 'I must go back to my friends, but I'd love to have a chance to chat later. So nice to meet you, Joanna.'

Her discomfort increased by a steely glance from Luc, Jo hoped her smile appeared genuine and unfeigned.

Everyone there seemed to know Luc; as waiters circulated with champagne and delicious nibbles a stream of people came up, and she was subjected to surveys that varied from veiled to avid. Like zookeepers viewing a rare animal for the first time, she thought, her sense of humour rescuing her.

Meticulously, Luc introduced them, mentioning that she owned her own skincare company.

Clever Luc. The topic interested everyone, and her feeling of dislocation began to ease.

Finally, some invisible signal indicated it was time to move. Luc took her arm, smiled down at her and said, 'Well done.'

'Thank you.' She hoped her smile showed no hint of challenge. 'What a lot of friends you have.'

His brows lifted. 'Not that many,' he told her. 'How many people do you call friends?'

And when she went to answer, he said coolly, 'Not acquaintances, or even people you like— but real friends? The sort you can ring at midnight and even if they're in bed with their latest lover they'll forgive you.'

Startled, Jo looked up, saw a glimmer of humour in the grey eyes and had to smile. 'None,' she said, dead-pan.

His smile set her heart singing. 'So what do you call a true friend?' he asked. 'Someone you can trust implicitly?'

'One who'll listen for an hour to me complaining when a new formula brings me out in a rash,' she said smartly.

His brows shot up. 'Has that happened?'

'Once. Turns out I'm allergic to one of the ingredients.' Jo totted up her friends, admitting, 'Actually, I can only think of three who'd listen for any more than twenty minutes. So I guess that gives me three good friends.'

'You're lucky,' he observed.

She stared at him. 'Yes, I suppose I am,' she said slowly. 'How about you?'

'One,' he said laconically.

Jo wasn't surprised. He didn't seem a man who'd give his trust easily, and a life spent in the cut-throat world of big business would have honed his formidable self-sufficiency.

Looking across the banqueting room, she caught Natasha Kidd's rapidly averted gaze and stifled an odd sense of foreboding. Was she Luc's lover?

Not yet, Jo thought, recollecting the hunger beneath the other woman's lashes as she'd looked up at him. But possibly she had hopes, and saw Jo as an obstacle.

Jo wished she could tell her that any relationship she had with Luc was safe. But it was none of her business, and she had no right to interfere.

The evening was well run, the food magnificent, and in spite of Luc's reservations the beautiful comedienne proved both extremely funny and very clever. Their table companions were interesting and kept their curiosity within bearable limits. Again Luc mentioned her business, and to her delight one woman extolled the worth of her products.

And the amount donated to the charity exceeded expectations enough to cause excitement and applause.

A very glamorous evening, Jo thought when it was over. So why was she glad to be leaving?

She thrust the thought from her mind to concentrate on smiling and nodding as they moved through the crowd. Luc moderated his long strides and exchanged the odd word with various acquaintances, but made sure he didn't stop.

Natasha Kidd was nowhere in evidence, thank heavens.

Outside it was raining, harbinger of a tropical depression that had the north of New Zealand in its sights. Staring straight ahead as they drove across the Harbour Bridge, Jo thought how alarmingly intimate it was to be cocooned in warmth and dryness with Luc when outside the lights dazzled and flared in the rain.

'Tired?'

She shook her head. 'Not at all.'

'Did you enjoy yourself?' A note in his voice made her cautious.

After a moment's thought, she said, 'It was very interesting.'

His laugh startled her. 'I've seldom heard less enthusiastic praise.'

She shrugged. 'I didn't know anyone there except you, but everyone was pleasant, the dresses were stunning and the food was delicious. Didn't you enjoy yourself?'

'Mostly,' he said, almost as though startled by his admission.

Jo couldn't help wondering why.

But that thought went out of her head completely when she checked her email after she'd showered and got ready for bed. One from Meru in Rotumea made her heart jolt.

I'll contact you at ten tomorrow morning on the video—it's important.

CHAPTER SEVEN

Jo STARED INTO the darkness, listening to rain that became heavier as the night wore on. Shards of confused dreams buzzed through her head—surely caused by Meru's ominous message, but somehow dominated by Luc's imposing presence. He'd just kissed her again…

No! She forced her wayward brain away from the memories. Worrying about Meru's message would play infinitely less havoc with her emotions than reliving those fevered moments. Even dreams of Luc's kisses had the power to set her pulse soaring.

Meru didn't flap easily, so whatever she had to discuss was not going to be good news.

The night seemed to drag on for ever, but eventually she fell asleep and dreamed again, waking to a dull light glimmering through the curtains. Rain beat against the windows, driven by a gale off the sea. Hastily she leapt out, but of course it was too early—Meru would still be in bed.

Still, there was work she could be doing. She opened the link on the computer, biting her lip as she waited for it to come through.

Nothing happened.

Angrily she stabbed at the keys, until a peal of thunder made her close down the computer and hastily switch off the power, grimacing in resignation. This tropical depression probably reached all the way from New Zealand to Rotumea, so it was more than likely there'd be no power on the island. So the communications system would be down.

Sighing, she accepted she'd have to possess her soul in patience, as her aunt would have said. Shower first, she decided, and then try again to see if Meru could get through.

But she'd only got halfway across the room when a noise erupted into the drumming of the rain—a violent crack that made Jo jump, and then a loud sighing crash.

'What—?' she gasped, swivelling towards the window.

She'd just pushed back the curtains when a knock on the door reminded her she was still in her nightgown, an elderly shift that finished at mid-thigh and was too transparent to be decent.

'Wait—I won't be a moment,' she called, and grabbed her dressing gown, also of faded cotton, though marginally less see-through than her gown.

She opened the door a fraction, her heart flipping when she saw Luc. 'What is it?' she asked.

Another bolt of lightning lit up Luc's unshaven face, followed by thunder rolling across the heavens.

'What happened?' she demanded.

'It sounds as though a tree's come down,' Luc said grimly, and strode into the room as the lights snapped off.

Together they peered out into the grey murk.

'Over there.' He pointed. 'On the beach front.'

Jo craned her head. Yesterday a large conifer had blocked the view of the outer harbour, but now she saw tossing, roiling waves as they pounded onto the shore.

'The Norfolk Island pine,' Luc said curtly. 'I'll collect Sanders and we'll make sure no one was walking past when it got struck.'

'I'll come with you.' She turned away, but Luc caught her arm.

As though on cue, lightning flashed again, and thunder rumbled like a distant cannon. Jo froze and for a moment the sound of the storm faded into nothingness against the reckless drumming of her heart.

Something kindled in Luc's hard eyes, but he dropped his hand and said harshly, 'You'd better get dressed.'

'All right.' Colour burned up from her breasts, and she took a step towards the wardrobe.

He went on, 'But stay inside. There's no need for you to get wet.' And you'd only be in the way, his tone implied.

Jo bristled, then managed to calm down. He knew this place; she didn't. More moderately she said, 'All right. But if I can help, let me know.'

'I will.'

He left then and she fled to the dressing room, closing the door behind her with a bang that echoed the drumming of her heart—only to have to open it again as she realised that without power she couldn't see.

How did Luc have that effect on her? Even with the door open the window provided hardly enough light to dress by, but she stripped off her night-clothes and dressing gown and hauled on a T-shirt and trousers, resenting that now familiar, wilful excitement that ached through her like an addictive drug.

The scream of a chainsaw cut through the keening of the storm, bringing her back to the window. Red lights were flashing from the road; someone had turned on a car's hazard lights as a warning.

They were soon joined by other lights as emergency services arrived, but the trees on the boundary prevented her from seeing what was happening, and the persistent, inexorable rain kept her inside, pacing restlessly around her room and trying hard to think of anything other than Meru's email.

Half an hour after the power had been restored she still couldn't contact Rotumea. She had to content herself with sending an email making another time for a video conference with her manager, before going downstairs.

Sanders appeared silently and sketched a small smile. 'Good morning. Breakfast is ready if you are. Mr MacAllister asked me to tell you not to wait for him.'

She was drinking coffee when Luc's voice brought her to her feet. After a moment's hesitation Jo went out of the room, stopping when she saw Sanders coming along the hall.

'I thought I heard Luc,' she said.

He allowed himself a small smile. 'Mr MacAllister is in the mudroom getting out of his wet-weather gear.' He indicated a hallway. 'Second door on the right.'

Mudroom? After a second's hesitation, Jo headed for the second door. Luc was shrugging out of a waterproof jacket, his hair darkened and glossy against his head, his features somehow made more pronounced by the shadow of his beard.

He looked up as she came in and his eyes narrowed. 'What's the matter?'

'Nothing,' she said automatically, wondering if her restlessness was painted in large letters on her face. She held out her hand and took the wet coat from him. 'I can't get through to Rotumea. How is it outside?'

'Give me that.' He whipped the coat from her and turned to hang it up, giving her an excellent view of broad shoulders dampened by rain.

The room suddenly seemed far too small and she wished she hadn't come. Why had she?

Because she wanted to make sure he was all right.

How stupid was that!

Hastily she said, 'I wondered if the tree had fallen near any houses.'

'It missed the nearest place by a few feet, although it gave everyone there a hell of a fright. They were lucky. We've cleared enough off the road for traffic to get through now.'

'That's good,' she said, hoping her expression was as cool as his.

He frowned. 'You look a bit wan. Did the rain keep you awake?'

'No,' she said too abruptly.

'Then what did?' He reached out to trace the skin beneath her eyes with a fingertip. 'These dark circles weren't caused by *nothing*.'

He hadn't moved any closer, but his touch set an exquisite anticipation singing through her. Her breath locked in her throat and she couldn't move, couldn't think of anything other than Luc's dark face, intent and purposeful as he scrutinised her.

She swallowed and managed to produce something she hoped sounded like her usual voice. 'I just had a restless night.'

'So did I,' he said, his voice suddenly harsh. 'I wonder if it's for the same reason.'

Jo squelched a nervous urge to lick her lips. 'Who knows?' she said, and managed to summon enough motivation to move back a step. 'You'd better have a shower before you start to get cold.'

His mouth quirked upwards. 'See you later, then.'

Stiff-shouldered, Jo walked away, hoping he

didn't realise just how strongly his male cha-risma affected her.

But how could he not? Luc was experienced; Tom had told her once that he'd been a target for women ever since he'd arrived at puberty.

Everything about him proclaimed a man who accepted the elemental power of his masculin-ity, just as he accepted his brilliant brain and formidable character. He deserved more than to be a target—a horrible term. It made her feel ashamed of being a woman. He deserved a wife who'd love him.

Where had that thought come from?

Jo shook her head impatiently. She was being idiotic. Luc MacAllister would do exactly what he wanted when it came to choosing a woman to marry. She had her own pressing concerns to deal with right now. Crossing her fingers, she took refuge in her room.

And heaved a huge sigh of relief when at last Meru's face appeared on the screen before her—a relief that rapidly dissolved after one look told her to brace herself.

'What's wrong?' she blurted.

Without preamble Meru said, 'I heard some-thing from my cousin yesterday that is…a prob-lem. You know my cousin Para'iki?'

'Yes, of course.' He was a chief. Jo's stomach tightened in anticipation of a blow.

'Jo, the Council have received an offer for the plant essence—with much more money than we are paying.'

'Did he say how much—and who was it from?'

Frowning, Meru said, 'I don't know how much, but more—he said a lot more. As for who—' She gave the name of a worldwide cosmetic and skincare concern owned by a huge corporate entity.

'Why them?' Jo said shakily. 'They cater to the mid-stream market, not to ours. Why do they want the essence? It's scarce and it's expensive...'

'I don't know, but it seems to me that if they are now deciding to expand into the upper bracket of the market, this would be a good way to do it.'

'Yes, of course.' Jo let out a long breath. 'Does Para'iki have any idea how the other chiefs feel about this?'

Meru sighed. 'Nobody will know until they have finished discussing it, and that could—*will*—take weeks,' she said dolefully. 'It is not a thing to be decided without much thought and care—you know that.'

No, the decision wouldn't be made lightly. The chiefs had to take a lot more into consideration than their verbal agreement with her. They had to plan for the future of Rotumea and its people.

Meru said worriedly, 'My cousin said to tell only you and to ask that you tell no one else until the decision is made.'

Jo swallowed. 'Of course I won't.'

The older woman said, 'He also said that Tom signed a paper with them when you were setting up the business; do you know what that was?'

Startled, Jo asked, 'A paper? Do you mean a legal document?'

'I think it must have been, or perhaps not—they would need nothing legal from Tom, his word was enough. But my cousin thought it would do no harm to remind the Council what Tom had promised...'

Tom had spoken for her during the negotiation process, but as far as Jo knew that was all he'd done. Her bewilderment growing, she said, 'I don't know anything—haven't heard anything—about a document. Tom certainly didn't mention it.'

'But perhaps you should look for one.' Meru sounded troubled. 'He was very respected, Jo. It is probably not important, but it might be.'

'I will.' Although it was foolish to hope that

somehow there might be something that would save the day. Tom's papers had gone to the solicitor, who'd surely have let her know if anything concerned her, but she'd check. Just in case…

She produced a smile. 'Meru, thanks so much for letting me know. Please thank your cousin for me too. And remember—whatever happens, you and everyone on Rotumea will be fine.'

'Yes, but what about you?'

'I'll manage,' Jo said as confidently as she could. 'Don't worry about me.'

But when she'd closed the link she sat with her eyes closed while thoughts tumbled through her brain, each one heavier with foreboding than the last.

Only for a moment, however. After a ragged breath she stood, exhaled and took in a painful breath, then straightened her shoulders. Worrying wasn't going to help. First she needed to concentrate on keeping the business going. And then she should make plans in case the chiefs decided against her.

And once she got back to Rotumea she'd look for that document, if it existed, even though she couldn't see how anything Tom had signed or written could possibly make a difference.

Logically, a huge corporation could offer a much better deal than she had, even if she used all of Tom's legacy when it was finally hers. He'd warned her that relying on a verbal agreement was dangerous, although he'd acknowledged that on Rotumea it was common practice. Had that mysterious piece of paper been some sort of safeguard?

As soon as she got back to Rotumea she'd look for this document—if it existed.

But oh, it would be heartbreaking to give up the business she'd created and worked so hard for.

A sharp knock snapped her head around. Pinning a smile to her lips, she walked across and opened her door.

Luc's intent gaze searched her face. With an authority that sparked instant resistance in Jo, he demanded, 'What's worrying you?'

She lifted her chin. 'It's got nothing to do with you.'

His brows climbed. 'I'm taking that as a refusal to discuss the matter.'

And not liking it, judging by his tone. Had no one ever refused him before?

Jo clamped her lips on the smart answer that sprang to mind. It would be stupid—downright foolhardy—to add to the mixture of emotions and sensations he aroused in her.

As calmly as she could, she told him, 'It's just something I have to deal with.'

'Does it concern the young cub who made an idiot of himself over you on Rotumea?' His voice didn't alter, but his eyes were hooded.

For a moment she didn't realise who he was talking about. Sean had receded into a distant past. Memory jolted into action, she said shortly, 'No, it has absolutely nothing to do with him. It's not personal.'

And parried another piercing scrutiny until, apparently satisfied, Luc nodded. 'Your business, then.' And before she could answer, he finished, 'All right. There's obviously a problem, so if you want to talk it over, I'm available.'

'Thank you.' Luc's disconcerting way of swinging from autocratic command to something approaching support unsettled her.

And warmed her dangerously.

Possibly after six months she'd be used to it. An odd pang of regret hit her. If only they'd met as strangers, without his preconceptions of her relationship to Tom affecting his attitude...

Stupid, stupid, *stupid*! If it weren't for Tom they'd never have met at all—in normal life they moved in circles so distant they might as well live in different galaxies.

But she wished Tom had told her more about

his stepson. Understanding Luc would have helped her, given her some guidelines on how to deal with the situation, instead of groping blindly, fighting against an attraction that was doomed to frustration.

Luc said, 'What are you thinking?'

How was he able to read her mind? Shaken, she said hastily, 'This whole business—you, me, enforced togetherness—is weird. Even though I know it's useless, I can't help wondering why Tom insisted on it.'

Luc bit back a short answer and said more temperately, 'It's quite simple. All his life Tom succeeded at doing exactly what he wanted, and I expect he couldn't resist extending his influence after his death.'

And watched with a sardonic amusement as her head came up and that firm chin angled in challenge.

'Whenever we talk about him we seem to be speaking of two different people,' she said, her gaze steady.

The way she idolised his stepfather was beginning to rub some unsuspected sensitivity in him to the edge of rawness. Luc resisted the urge to tell her to grow up, to accept that men behaved differently to the women who shared their bed.

Especially if they were young and lovely...

Into his mind there danced the image of her that morning, with her magnificent mane of hair tousled around her face above shabby night-clothes. He'd like to see her in satin, or something silken that clung lovingly to her breasts and revealed her long, elegant legs. His breath quickened as he imagined running his hands through that hair, turning her face up to his...

Clamping down on a savagely primal response, he said, 'You're twenty-three, aren't you?'

She lifted startled eyes to meet his. 'Yes. What has that to do with anything?'

'It's old enough, I'd have thought, to realise that people present a different face to every person.'

Jo thought about that for a moment, before returning sweetly, 'That's a huge generalisation, and do you have the research to back it up?'

Taken by surprise, he laughed. 'Spoken like a true scientist. No, but if it's been done I'll find it. I'm giving you the benefit of my experience.'

'Very cynical experience,' she shot back, daring him with another swift tilt of her chin.

Luc could see why Tom had been intrigued by her—apart from the physical allure of young curves and burnished skin, of course. She'd have been a challenge, and Tom enjoyed challenges.

conceit.' She allowed herself a small smile before adding wryly, 'But very, *very* intimidating.'

'And gorgeous,' her friend supplied with a grin. 'Are you going to try your luck with him?'

'Do I look like an idiot?' Jo demanded, hoping her tone hid the embarrassment that heated her skin.

'No, but you're blushing.' Lindy laughed. 'Go on, admit you fancy him something rotten.'

'He's not my type,' Jo told her, picking up her teacup and hiding behind it.

'What's that got to do with anything?' Lindy asked. 'I never thought Kyle was your type either—he was too selfish—but you fell for him.'

'And look where that got me,' Jo said grimly.

Lindy knew of Kyle's betrayal. 'He was a louse,' she agreed. 'Charming and witty and great fun, and selfish to the core. I bet he wanted you to put your mother in a home.'

Jo bit her lip. 'Yes,' she said tonelessly.

'And when you wouldn't he slept with Faith Holden to punish you. I know you were shattered when he walked out, but I'm sure you realise now you're well out of it.'

'Of course I do.' Jo set her cup down. 'But Luc MacAllister is nothing like Kyle—and we don't have that sort of relationship anyway.'

'He was watching you that night at the resort

As did he.

'I don't consider myself a cynic,' he said coolly. 'I've learnt to be careful in relationships, but that happens to most of us, I imagine.'

Shrugging away the memory of a previous lover, paid to rave to a magazine about his prowess in bed, he said, 'Once most people get past adolescence they guard against flinging themselves into relationships without first making sure both parties understand the implications and expectations.'

She pulled a face. 'You make love sound like a business deal.'

'Love, no. It's marriage that's the business deal,' he said cynically.

She gave him a long, assessing stare. 'I bet you'd insist any future wife sign a pre-nuptial agreement.'

'Of course.' Too many promising entrepreneurs—including several mentored by Tom—had been burned by reckless marriages that ended in acrimony, forced to sell up to provide a former spouse with unearned income for the rest of her life.

He awaited her answer with anticipation.

'Actually, I think I probably would too.' She smiled. 'Although I've never considered it before, it does seem a sensible precaution.'

In any other woman in her situation he'd appreciate and understand such pragmatism. For some reason, in Jo it irritated him. For a moment he surprised himself by wondering what she'd be like in the throes of a heartfelt love, prepared to offer herself without thought of profit.

Cold, hard reality told him it would never happen. He doubted that such unconditional love existed. Even if it did, any woman who'd taken a man forty years older as a lover, bartering her body for the prospect of gain, was far too cold-blooded to allow herself to fall wildly in love. Joanna had made a very good show of shock when she'd discovered how much she'd inherited, but her chagrin at the condition in Tom's will revealed her true emotions. She'd expected the money to be hers immediately, to spend as she wished.

He owed it to Tom to make sure she learned how to take care of her inheritance, but once the six months was up she'd be able to do what she liked with it.

Yet somehow he couldn't see her squandering it.

Of course, plenty of courtesans had been excellent businesswomen…

He said coolly, 'Anyone who doesn't insist on a pre-nup is an idiot.'

With a look from beneath her lashes—a look she probably practised in front of her mirror— she said, 'I'll keep that in mind.'

No doubt of that, Luc thought caustically. He said, 'I'll be out for the rest of the day. What are your plans?'

'If this rain eases I'm going to spend the afternoon with a friend in Devonport,' she told him. 'You've seen her—I was with Lindy and her husband the night we…ah…met.'

He nodded. 'Do you have a current New Zealand driver's license?'

'Yes. But Lindy's coming to pick me up.'

He nodded. 'OK, then. I'll see you tonight.'

The rain did ease, although it didn't stop while Jo spent the day catching up with her friend in the small flat Lindy and her new husband were renting.

'Until we can save the deposit on a house Lindy said cheerfully. She grinned at Jo. 'N everyone has your luck! Fancy living wi tycoon in a huge, flash mansion on the p est and most private beach on the North What's he like?'

Jo didn't need to think. 'Formidable

'Full of himself? Arrogant? Intimi

'Not arrogant, and I haven't seen a

on Rotumea,' Lindy persisted. 'And you were very conscious of him too.'

'He knew who I was, of course. I suppose he was checking me out.' She grinned. 'Though if he was watching anyone, it was you. You looked fantastic.'

'Honeymoons do that for you.' Lindy's infectious laugh rang out. 'You should try one some time. Seriously, you haven't let Kyle put you off men completely, have you?'

'Of course not,' Jo said firmly, ignoring the apprehension that contracted her stomach muscles. 'But right now I'm having too much fun with my business to spare the time for any sort of relationship, especially one as big as marriage.'

'Well, enjoy your stay with Mr Gorgeous Tycoon. And don't try to fool me into thinking you're not just the teeniest bit lusting after him, because I won't believe you.'

'I'm not into wasting my time,' Jo said a little shortly. 'He's had a couple of serious affairs—one with that stunningly beautiful model Annunciata Someone, and the other was with the almost as stunning Mary Heard, who writes those brilliant thrillers. Clearly he likes beauties in his bed, and I know my limitations.'

'You might not be model-beautiful, but you've

got style,' Lindy said loyally. 'Anyway, I'm not suggesting you fall in love with the man—that would really be asking for trouble.'

Jo looked at her with affection. 'Exactly,' she said. 'Don't worry about me—I'm not planning to do anything at all for six months but cope with Luc MacAllister as best I can, and run my business.'

'OK, but you're selling yourself short. Even if you don't want to fall in love with the man, I bet he's fantastic in bed.' She fanned her cheek with one hand and laughed at Jo's startled face. 'Don't look so shocked—marriage hasn't stopped me appreciating an alpha male!'

What startled Jo was the jealousy that ripped through her—a fierce, quite unwarranted possessiveness she'd never experienced before.

Lindy sighed. 'Funny how a woman just knows, isn't it? Some men just kind of reek of sex appeal, and they don't even have to be handsome—although it helps if they look as good as your tycoon. I wonder what clues us into it?'

'I don't know, and I'm not going there,' Jo said cheerfully. She glanced at her watch and said, 'I'd better go, Lindy.'

'Oh, stay for dinner. We can run you home afterwards, and it would be so nice to have dinner with you.'

Jo hesitated. 'I don't have a key,' she said, 'so I'd have to be back at a reasonable hour.'

'That's not a problem. We're early birds. My beloved gets up at some ungodly hour in the morning to run umpteen kilometres before breakfast. Should you let someone know?'

Sanders took the news with his usual taciturnity, and they organised for her to be home by ten. Smiling, she told Lindy, 'He sounded just like my mother used to.'

Lindy said with awe, 'Your Luc has a *manservant*?'

'He's not mine! And it's Tom's house—*was* Tom's house—so I guess Sanders was Tom's employee.'

'Good heavens... Is he a kind of valet?'

'I don't think so—more a general factotum and cook, which he does extremely well. The whole set-up is way out of our league, Lindy.'

Just before ten that night Sanders opened the door to her and said, 'Good evening.'

Jo acknowledged him and turned to wave Lindy and her husband goodbye. 'Thank you, Sanders. I wonder when this rain is going to stop.'

'Not for another couple of days, according to the weather forecast.' Sanders ushered her inside. 'It's a very slow-moving tropical depression. They're forecasting floods in the upper North Island tomorrow.'

He paused, then said, 'Mr MacAllister isn't at home yet. He rang to say he'd be late. Is there anything I can get you?'

'No, thanks,' she said, stifling a suspicious regret.

Up in her room she showered and got into her night-clothes, then sat down at the computer. Nothing from Rotumea... Sighing with frustration, she closed the computer down.

Not that she expected any news so soon, but it irked her to be away at this delicate time. She had no doubt Meru and Savisi would be lobbying tactfully for her, but she really needed to be there herself.

Tom, you really made a mess of this, she thought dismally, getting up to wander across to the window. Of course he couldn't have foreseen this particular situation, but the offer to the chiefs had come at the very worst moment.

Conservative to a man, the members of the Council would be more likely to listen to their relatives who worked for her, but even so... She should be there, planning strategy.

The conversation with Meru echoed through her mind. Papers...

Some small door in her brain popped open.

'Of course!' she breathed, closing the curtains and turning back to the room.

If Tom had hidden papers she knew where they'd be—in the old Chinese chest where he kept his precious whisky.

He'd shown her the secret panel once, laughing when she'd expressed dismay that it was empty.

Perhaps there was now something in it...

She wasn't going to sleep tonight. The hours stretched ahead of her, filling her with tormenting fears that drove her downstairs to a bookcase in what Luc called the morning room.

It contained an eclectic selection of books ranging from bestsellers to local histories, one of which she chose. Clutching it, she tiptoed back up the stairs and had just opened her bedroom door when she heard a sound behind her.

Every sense springing into full alert, she stopped and swivelled around. Luc was a few paces behind her, saturnine in his black and white evening clothes. He looked...magnificent.

And vaguely menacing. Feeling oddly foolish, she swallowed and scanned his unreadable expression, heat flooding her skin. 'Oh. Hello. I went down for a book.'

'And have you found what you were looking for?' he enquired coolly.

CHAPTER EIGHT

LUC'S VOICE WAS deeper than normal, the words almost guttural. His gaze, narrowed and darkening in the semi-gloom of the hall, never left Jo's face. She saw heat in the depths of his eyes, and something else—a keenness her body reacted to with a sharp, frightening hunger.

Run! Every nerve and muscle tensed at the instinctive warning. Like a shield, she held up the book so that he could see it. 'Yes, thank you,' she said too rapidly, clumsily half-turning in an attempt to escape his penetrating scrutiny.

Her heart was hammering so loudly she was sure Luc could hear it, and a delicious, tempting weakness dazzled her mind.

Run—run while you can...

Yet her body resisted the command from her brain, refusing to obey even when Luc reached out to rest the tip of one long finger on the traitorous pulse at the base of her throat.

Eyes holding hers, he asked in that roughened voice, 'Are you afraid?'

Without volition, Jo shook her head. 'Of you?' Her voice was husky and low. 'No.'

'Good.'

If she'd heard nothing more than satisfaction in the single word she might have found the self-possession to pull away. But it seemed torn from his throat, raw with desire, as though he too had fought this since their gazes had clashed in the sultry, scented warmth of a tropical night.

It's too soon, the nagging voice of caution insisted. For once, Jo wasn't listening—didn't want to hear. Her whole being was concentrated on the subtle caress of Luc's finger while it slid from the pulse in her throat down to the first button of her loose shift.

Her breath came faster, keeping time with her heart, with her racing blood, with the emotions and sensations that surged through her, catapulting her into a place she'd never been before.

She craved Luc with a hunger powerful enough to wash away everything but that blazing need. And this time she didn't try to fool herself, as she had with Kyle. This wasn't love. She expected nothing more from Luc than fulfilment of desire, the unchaining of the passion—

intoxicating, compelling and intense—that had been smouldering inside her.

He was experienced enough to discern the need flashing through her. In a rigidly controlled voice he asked, 'Joanna, is this what you want?'

For a second, a heartbeat, she wavered.

Until he bent his head and kissed the smooth skin his hand had revealed, his mouth a brand against her sensitive flesh, his subtle, fresh male scent overwhelming her feeble defences.

'Joanna?'

His lips against her skin were exquisite, shocking. Her breasts lifted when she dragged in a breath and muttered, 'Yes.'

He gave a smothered groan and lifted his head and kissed her mouth, and she surrendered. Luc kissed her as though he was dying for her, as though she had been lost to him and was now found again—as though he had longed for her during too many hopeless years...

And she kissed him back, glorying in his hunger, in the powerful force of his body, in the sensual magic they made together.

And then Luc lifted his head and demanded, 'Are you protected?'

Stunned, she stared at him, saw his eyes harden, and he said curtly, 'Tell me.'

Jo bit back a wild urge to lie. 'No. No, I'm not.'

He said something beneath his breath, something she heartily agreed with, and let her go.

'I don't have anything either,' he said.

Shivering, she stood still while the rain poured down outside, the sound of tears, of pain and loneliness. Her fierce physical frustration gave way to bleak humiliation.

It took every ounce of courage she possessed to mutter, 'I'll go, then,' and turn blindly towards the door.

'Joanna—'

She shook her head. 'No, leave it at that,' she said, fumbling for the handle. It wouldn't open and she flinched when his hand covered hers and twisted the opposite way.

For a few seconds his warmth enfolded her, his grip tightening as though he didn't want to release her, and then the door gave way and he stepped back.

Shaking inwardly, she shot through the door and turned to close it, forcing herself to look up as she searched for words to say that might break the tension. None came.

In the darkness he seemed even taller, looming like some image from a dream.

'It's all right,' he said, each word level and cold. 'I can control my baser urges, if that's what you're afraid of.'

Her chin came up. 'I'm not.' She refused to admit even to herself that she wished—oh, for just a second—that Luc MacAllister wasn't always in control.

With a sting in her voice, she said, 'And I thought calling desire a base urge had departed with the Victorians. Goodnight, Luc.'

The door closed firmly, its small click barely audible above the renewed thudding of the rain.

Luc turned and headed for his own room, cursing his unruly body.

And his stupidity in not making sure he'd been prepared. He knew why; he'd been confident of his immunity. The fact that Jo had been his stepfather's mistress should have quenched his dangerous, unwelcome hunger.

But when he'd held her, kissed her, all he'd thought of was taking her, of making slow, deliberate love to her until she forgot every man she'd ever had before him, until she was lost in her own need.

For him.

Had she been faking it? He strode into his bedroom and switched on the light, his expression set and hard. He didn't think so—and in his youth he'd gained enough experience of the wiles of women to judge whether their passion was real or assumed.

Desire could be faked, but that delicate shudder he'd felt beneath his hand, the heat of her exquisite skin on his palm, the rapid throbbing of the pulse in her throat, the widening of her eyes as she'd looked up at him—all spoke of real hunger.

So, she wanted him.

Making love to her would have rid him of this itch, because that was all it was—nothing personal, merely a primitive heat in the blood. Calling it anything else would be giving it an importance it didn't possess.

But they had to spend six months together. Making love to Joanna would be stupid for so many reasons...

He walked across to the windows and looked out at the rain. He'd like to be somewhere wild right now, watching waves crash against cliffs.

The memory of Joanna's face as she'd closed the door against him played across his mind. Seductive lips, made a little more sensuous by his kiss, the smoky depths of her eyes half-hidden by long lashes, the faint, elusive fragrance of her warm satin skin...

His body hardened, his hunger so powerful he had to lock every muscle to stop himself from swivelling and walking back to her room. His hands folded into fists at his sides.

Control of his life had been wrenched from him. The months ahead loomed like a term of imprisonment or a journey into forbidden territory.

Tom, you bastard, just why the hell did you set this up? What was going through your devious mind when you designed that will?

When Jo woke the rain had stopped. She blinked at the brilliance that glowed through the curtains, colour burning through her skin as memories swarmed back—of Luc holding her against his powerful, aroused body…and the erotic dreams her untrammelled mind had conjured during her sleep.

She wanted Luc with something like desperation. It was all very well to realise that going to bed with him would have been the most stupid, reckless, dangerous thing she could have done.

Her body didn't agree.

Driven by restlessness, she got up and pulled back the curtains, trying to be grateful for the iron control that had put an end to their lovemaking.

Respect wasn't something she'd expected from Luc, but it seemed he respected her decision that the game wasn't worth the candle.

And in turn she owed him respect for his instant acceptance.

With Kyle it had been different—he'd been eager for sex almost immediately, calling her an ice maiden when she'd refused. He'd insisted that he'd make sure nothing happened. She'd been steadfast, and later he'd laughed about it, telling her his words had been angry because he'd loved her so much, and her refusal had seemed cold and unfeeling...

Like an idiot she'd believed him. She should have guessed then that for Kyle his own needs came first.

She stared down at the glinting, dancing water in the big pool. Working with figures was her least favourite part of being a businesswoman, but she needed that discipline right now. Not only would it drive away the memories that fogged her brain with delicious thoughts of Luc's passion, it would force her to concentrate on what was really important.

But before she started on the accounts she'd ring Lindy, get the name of her doctor and see if she could wangle an appointment.

For a moment she wavered. Wouldn't getting protection make her more vulnerable to the hunger prowling through her?

What if somehow she found herself in Luc's

arms again—surely it would be easier to keep her head if she was faced with the prospect of pregnancy?

Not going to happen, she thought stoutly as she pulled on her bikini and wrapped a sarong around her. Now that she knew how susceptible she was to Luc she'd be forewarned. Getting protection would simply be a sensible precaution—one both her mother and her aunt had insisted was the mark of a responsible woman.

Ignoring a treacherous flutter in the pit of her stomach, she picked up a towel and a change of clothes. Something told her that the silent Sanders would not approve of wet people wandering through the house, so there was bound to be a cabana or pool-room—whatever they called such an amenity.

There was. Sanders himself showed her how to get there. And very luxurious it was too—as immaculate as the rest of the house. Nothing like the house on Rotumea, she thought, aching with sudden grief. This place had been decorated by someone with exquisite taste. The house on Rotumea hadn't been decorated at all—Tom had just bought what he liked.

Dismay gripped her when she realised Luc had beaten her to the pool, tanned arms cutting incisively through the water, wet hair slicked into darkness. When he saw her he stood up.

Jo swallowed. He was too much—all sleek, burnished skin with the long, powerful muscles of an athlete. Hastily she said, 'Oh, hi. Great minds and all that…'

His expression was unreadable. 'I'll be out in a moment,' he said, almost as though conveying a favour.

'No need. I don't take up much room.'

He raised his brows but said nothing before diving back under.

Possibly exorcising the same demon she'd been wrestling with all night—a physical frustration so intense it burned. Jo dived in neatly and began to swim lengths too, determined to ignore the image of broad, water-slicked shoulders and chest—and the tormenting memories of how secure she'd felt in his arms…

She swam with steady strokes, forcing herself to focus on counting laps, hugely relieved when Luc hauled himself out.

The sun beat down with gathering heat, but she kept swimming until Luc called from the side, 'Breakfast.'

'Coming.' She finished the length before climbing out.

Even in a short-sleeved shirt and light trousers, he looked tall and powerful, very much in command.

Made uneasy by his unsmiling regard, she walked briskly towards him.

'It's all right,' he said curtly. 'I'm not going to leap on you.'

'I know that,' she retorted, embarrassed by a stupid blush.

'You're not acting as though you believe it.'

To which she had no answer. 'I'll get dressed and be out shortly,' she told him and forced herself to walk at a slightly slower pace past him.

Her shower was the swiftest on record, although her fingers were clumsy as she pulled on her pareu and combed her hair back from her face, wishing it didn't curl so obstinately. The pareu clung to her damp skin, revealing bare shoulders and every curve of her body. Under Luc's hooded scrutiny, clothes that were normal everyday wear on Rotumea—her bikini, the pareu—somehow seemed to constitute an overt attempt at seduction.

She bared her teeth at her reflection, braced herself and went out, her head held high. Luc was standing in the shade of the jasmine sprawling across the pergola, talking into a cellphone, his brows drawn together.

He looked up and something flashed into his

eyes, a flaring recognition of what had passed between them the previous night. Her skin tightened.

This was not a good idea…

He said something sharp and conclusive into the phone, snapped it shut and strode towards her.

'You'll be cold,' he said. 'I keep forgetting you've spent years in the tropics.'

'Not that many. This is fine, but I'll sit in the sun instead of the shade.'

He nodded. 'I'll pull out the table.'

Before they sat down he asked, 'Are you wearing sunscreen?'

'Yes.' Skin like hers was very much at risk from New Zealand's unforgiving sunlight.

'So these freckles weren't caused by the sun?' He indicated her nose, where five pale gold dots lingered.

She stiffened, only relaxing when it was clear he wasn't going to touch her. 'They're relics from my childhood,' she told him. 'Even though my mother and aunt insisted I wear sunscreen all the time—and my aunt used to make me wear an island hat whenever I went outside in Rotumea—I still got freckles. These ones just don't want to go.'

'They're charming,' he said coolly. 'How do

you manage to achieve that faint sheen, as though you're sprinkled with gold dust?'

Heat flamed in the pit of her stomach. Trying for a light rejoinder, she said, 'I've called my freckles lots of things, but never charming. As a kid I hated them. As for gold dust—it's a pretty allusion, but the colour's entirely natural.' Keeping her gaze steady with an effort of will, she returned his scrutiny. 'You're lucky. That built-in Mediterranean tan must be a huge help in resisting the sun.'

'It is,' he said casually. 'I don't rely on it entirely, however.'

All very civilised, she thought as she picked up a napkin, sedately unfolding it into her lap.

Watching them, hearing them no one would know that last night they'd kissed like famished lovers...

He said, 'I'm going to ask a favour of you.'

'What sort of favour?' she asked warily.

'An easy one for you to carry out, I hope. I'm asking for your discretion. I'd rather you didn't divulge anything of Tom's will or your relationship with him while we're staying together.'

Whatever she'd expected, it wasn't this. Frowning, she said, 'I'm not ashamed of anything I've done, if that's what you think. And I'm not going to lie about—'

'I'm not asking you to lie,' he interrupted austerely, 'but there's bound to be gossip.' He indicated the table with a sweep of his hand. 'Help yourself—or Sanders can cook breakfast for you if you want. And if you'd like coffee, I'll have some too.'

'No, thanks.' She helped herself to cereal and fruit and yoghurt, and poured the coffee.

Luc resumed, 'There's already been speculation about your place in his life. It will make things less stressful for everyone if you refuse to discuss your relationships with him or with me.'

He was clearly bent on damping down that speculation, but she felt obliged to point out, 'Usually a "No Comment" is taken as confirmation. If anyone is rude enough to ask, I'll tell them the truth—that my aunt was his housekeeper, and after she died I took over her position.'

His brows rose. Had he expected her to resist? She said, 'But how do we explain my presence with you?'

'We don't,' he said calmly. 'We fly back to Rotumea once I get this mess here cleaned up.' He looked at her narrowly. 'You did well the other night.'

'I'm not entirely sure in what way,' she said

crisply, feeling sorry for whoever had created the mess he was dealing with.

He shrugged. 'It's called networking, and it's a necessary part of life when you're starting a business. Tom must have told you how important it can be.'

Sadly, she said, 'Yes. I wish he hadn't done this. It wasn't like him to leave things in such an ambiguous tangle.'

'He was always devious, but the stroke affected him.' Luc made no attempt to soften the blunt statement.

Reluctantly Jo nodded and drank a fortifying mouthful of coffee before saying, 'I need to be in Rotumea to run the business. It's very personal. Tom knows—*knew*—that. I'm sure he wouldn't have intended you to take me around like some…some extra piece of luggage!'

Luc leaned back in his chair and surveyed her. 'Tom was first and foremost an entrepreneur. He'd be thinking of the contacts you'd make.'

Exasperated, she demanded, 'And what contacts do *you* have in the world of skincare?'

'Very few, but I have a lot amongst those who use skincare. Witness those at the dinner that night.'

She looked up, and met a gaze that held cynical amusement. 'So that's why you mentioned my tiny business?'

'It's all part of the game,' Luc pointed out, not attempting to hide the cynical note in his voice. 'The demographic you're targeting has money. They frequent charity dinners, and by and large they're prepared to pay considerable sums for a good product.' His smile was brief, almost a taunt. 'I'm sure that anywhere I go you'll enjoy checking out spas and beauty shops and places like that.'

'If that was Tom's reasoning, he could have a point.' And because her voice shook a little, she asked, 'When do we go back to Rotumea?'

'I have probably three days' work here.'

Good—so she'd have a chance to get that prescription. 'Fine. I'll check out the day spa here that stocks and uses our product.'

'Will you be trying for more business?'

'Not in Auckland,' she said. 'In the demographic I'm targeting exclusivity is a big asset.'

'While you're here, do you have any relatives you want to contact?'

She shook her head. 'Not a one. How about you?'

His brows lifted. 'Several in France and Scotland—none here now Tom's gone. How did you manage to end up with so few?'

She shrugged. 'My mother and my aunt grew up in care. My father came from a very religious family—they didn't approve of Mum, and they certainly wouldn't have approved of her having his child out of wedlock. He was killed in a motorbike accident going to see her, and they blamed her. They never contacted her. I don't even know who they are.'

Brows knotted, he said in a hard voice, 'If that's the sort of people they are you're better off not knowing them.'

Jo was oddly touched by his sympathy. 'I don't miss them. And while we're here I'll put flowers on his grave.' With a challenging glance she finished, 'What about these Scottish and French relatives?'

And held her breath, wondering if he was going to tell her to mind her own business.

Instead he said evenly, 'My mother grew up in Provence in a half-ruined chateau. She had no siblings. She met and married my father— a Scottish gamekeeper—when she was visiting a school friend in the Highlands. It was a love match, but she couldn't cope with life there, and she returned to the chateau. I was born there. Five years later, after my father's death, she married Tom.'

He sounded like a policeman giving evidence,

the colourless summary doing nothing to allay Jo's curiosity. What he left out was intriguing. Had his mother's family owned that half-ruined chateau?

For some reason she felt a pang of sympathy for him. Squelching it, she said, 'A half-ruined chateau—how very romantic.'

He reached for his coffee. 'It's not ruined any longer,' he said indifferently.

'Does it belong to your family?'

'It belongs to me.'

She recalled Tom's wry comment that Luc's mother had wanted her son to marry into the French aristocracy. Because she'd been an aristocrat herself? So what had her family thought of her marriage to a gamekeeper? And of Luc himself, product of what they possibly felt was a misalliance?

Or not. After all, she knew very little about French aristocrats down on their luck, or tumbledown chateaux.

And nothing about Luc, except that he kissed like a demon lover, and that just looking at him set every cell in her body on fire...

'That's an interesting expression,' he said mockingly.

Flushing, and hoping she didn't sound defen-

sive, she said, 'I'm picturing a half-ruined chateau in Provence.'

'Once you get your hands on Tom's legacy
you'll be able to see as many as you like,' he told
her. 'In fact, that amount of money will probably buy one for you. It might even be enough
to turn the building into a liveable home instead
of a wreck, but there wouldn't be any change.'

'I'll be quite content to view from a distance,
like any other sightseer. And Tom's money will
go to growing the business.'

'How do you plan to conquer the cosmetics
world if the base ingredient in your products is
confined to only one small Pacific island?'

'As Pacific islands go, Rotumea is actually
quite large,' she returned. 'And there are other,
much more common ingredients we use too—
coconut water from green coconuts, coconut oil,
the essence from Rotumea's native gardenia.'
She met his eyes squarely. 'I haven't yet worked
out all the fine details of my plan to take over
the world of skincare, but when I do, I won't be
telling anyone about it.'

'Tom taught you well.' His smile was coolly
ironic.

It always came back to Tom.

Deliberately Jo relaxed her stiff shoulders.

What she and Tom had shared was precious to her. And she wasn't going to keep trying to convince Luc that his stepfather had never so much as touched her, beyond the occasional—very occasional and very brief—hug.

Just keep in mind how very judgemental Luc is, and you'll be safe, she told that weak inner part of her that melted whenever Luc's gunmetal gaze met hers.

She drank more coffee and said cheerfully, 'He had a lot to teach. I'll bet he was a help to you when you started.'

Luc gave a short, derisive laugh. 'Not Tom,' he said. 'He told me I'd learn far more if I made my own mistakes.'

Again she felt that strange sympathy. 'And did you?'

'I learnt enough to take his life's work away from him.'

Jo blinked and ventured, 'You had a reason.'

His wide shoulders lifted in an infinitesimal shrug. 'I did.' After a pause, he added, 'I told you he changed after the very minor stroke he had. Not vastly, not obviously, but there were... incidents. He made decisions that could have—in one case definitely would have—led to disaster. The man who built Henderson's from scratch would never have made such decisions, but Tom wouldn't admit or accept that he could make a mistake. He had the failings of his virtues, and his determination got in the way.'

Which put a different slant on events. She'd known Tom before that stroke, but only as a child and during the holidays. While she'd lived in Rotumea he'd had the occasional spurt of what she'd thought was slightly irrational behaviour, but as her aunt had taken the incidents without comment she'd assumed this was normal for him.

But as head of a huge organisation, with thousands of people dependent on his health and managerial skills, one wrong decision could cause chaos. Perhaps Luc had been justified in ousting him.

Of course, Luc could be lying…

One glance at his strong features changed her mind. Lying didn't fit him. His behaviour last night had convinced her of his fundamental honesty as well as his formidable self-control.

Of course, he might have been trying her out, not really wanting her…

She had to stop second-guessing—something Tom had taught her to do, only he'd called it seeing situations clearly and from every conceivable angle. In business it worked well, but she was beginning to feel that in personal life it wasn't so efficient.

'You don't believe me,' Luc said without rancour.

Of course, he didn't care what she thought of him.

'Actually, I do,' she said, keeping her voice level. 'I can't see Tom ever admitting to a weakness. As you say, he had the faults of his virtues.'

'At least he didn't fail in the generosity stakes,' Luc observed.

That hurt, but she said calmly, 'No, he didn't. Although, being Tom, he still insisted on having the final word. You and I are caught in a trap of his making, with no way out.'

Luc laughed without humour. 'I'm sure that thought gave him great—and certainly as far as I'm concerned—rather malicious pleasure.'

'Whereas I think he meant some good for both of us by it.' Still smarting from his remark about Tom's generosity, she couldn't resist adding, 'Possibly you'd know him better if you'd seen more of him.'

And immediately wished she hadn't. Luc's expression didn't alter, but she received a strong impression of emotions reined back, of anger.

He finished his coffee, pushed his plate away and said calmly, 'We were estranged for the last years of his life. He wouldn't see me after I took over. When my mother sided with me—because she'd noticed and been worried by the change in him—he saw it as a betrayal, and although they kept up a pretence, they didn't live together as man and wife after that.'

Ashamed, she said, 'I'm sorry, I shouldn't have said that.'

'Especially as you were presumably the reason he settled in Rotumea and forbade either of us—or any of his friends—from visiting him.'

Stunned by his caustic tone, she said, 'I most certainly was not!'

He got to his feet and shrugged. 'You must have been. And I despise him for choosing to use such a weapon against my mother.'

The cold contempt in his voice shrivelled something vital inside Jo, made her feel sick and angry at the same time. 'I don't believe he thought of any such thing.'

And immediately cursed herself for saying anything at all. She tried to make it better. 'He always spoke of your mother with affection and respect. And we were *not* lovers.' Passion—a violent need to force him to believe her—made her voice harsh. She blurted, 'The very idea makes me feel sick.'

No emotion showed in his face, in those hard

eyes, as he looked down at her. 'Your nausea obviously didn't worry Tom, or drive you away.' When she would have burst into speech again he held up his hand.

'Leave it, Joanna. Just leave it. He certainly wasn't the saint you seem to believe him to be.' His mouth twisted. 'And I can understand him. I've made it more than obvious I'm not immune to your not inconsiderable assets, so who am I to mock him? My mother was his age, and not well for the final years of her life. You must have been like a breath of fresh air to him, as well as a handy weapon.'

CHAPTER NINE

BACK IN ROTUMEA, Jo unpacked, then walked out onto the wide lanai. Sunlight streamed through the trees—so intense it looked like shimmering bars of gold in the salt-scented air. Her heart jolted when she realised Luc was gazing out to sea from the shade of a tangled thicket of palms.

It was all she could do to shield her hungry gaze. The past days in Auckland had been outwardly serene, but beneath it she'd been battling chaotic emotions. Luc's contempt hurt her more severely than Kyle's betrayal.

Facing that truth still terrified her.

Without preamble, she said, 'Would it be difficult for you to work with someone here? A housekeeper?'

Luc turned, brows drawing together. 'Not unless she talks.'

'She won't.' She expanded, 'The business is getting busy, and I'm going to be away most days.'

He nodded, although his gaze remained narrowed and keen. Colour warmed the skin over her cheekbones. Of course he knew why she was doing this.

He said, 'I'll pay her.' When she opened her mouth to protest he said curtly, 'At least you won't then feel obliged to offer me coffee or meals. And presumably you'll feel safer.'

Jo struggled to hide her chagrin. She'd hoped—uselessly—he wouldn't realise just how dangerously vulnerable she was. When Luc kissed her all self-control vanished, sweeping every vestige of common sense with it.

Heat burned up from her breasts, but before she could answer he went on, 'You obviously have someone in mind for the job.'

'My factory manager has a cousin who'll be perfect,' she told him.

Luc nodded. 'Organise her hours any way you want,' he said indifferently. 'I'll be away for the rest of the afternoon.'

Jo turned, relieved to be summoned to the house by the shrill call of the telephone.

Five minutes later she hung up, her gaze falling on the Chinese chest. Now was the perfect time to see if Tom had hidden something in the secret panel. Frowning, she pressed the centre of one of the mother-of-pearl flowers, letting out a sharp hiss of breath as the panel slid back.

'Yes!' she breathed triumphantly. It did hold something—not a thick wad, but definitely a couple of documents. One fell onto the floor; frowning, she picked it up.

A strange feeling of dislocation made her pause. 'Oh, don't be silly,' she said out loud. Fingers shaking a little, she unfolded it.

It was a copy of her birth certificate. Astonishment froze her into place as her gaze traced her father's name—so young to die, unknown to her except from a few faded photographs and her mother's loving recollections.

He'd been handsome, her mother had said, and kind. And funny. He was a mechanic; they'd been planning to marry when he'd been killed. Ilona hadn't known she was pregnant, and she'd been forbidden to attend his funeral by his parents, yet although her heart had been shattered she'd been so glad she carried his baby, so glad she had someone else to love, someone to take care of…

Why had Tom wanted a copy of her birth certificate?

Just another thing she'd never know, Jo thought drearily, and slid it underneath the small pile.

Looking at papers clearly never meant for her seemed too much like an intrusion. She sat down at the table, her fingers pleating and unpleating, until in the end she opened up the first sheet of paper.

It was the document Meru had told her about. A quick check revealed it was of no use to her— merely a note saying Tom guaranteed that her business would be conducted in a suitable manner.

She firmed her trembling lips. It was too much—the unexpected reference to her parents, the inevitable loss of her business—all of those she could cope with, but the constant tension of living with Luc had left her raw and fragile, as though she'd lost a layer of skin.

'Get over it,' she muttered and started to fold up the papers, saying something beneath her breath when one slipped out of the pile. She glanced at the heading as she picked it up and frowned again. It was from a medical laboratory in Sydney, Australia, and to her astonishment her name leapt out from it.

Stunned, she read it. Then, her hand shaking so much she dropped it, she picked up the document it had been folded with. Tom's handwriting leapt out at her. *Dear Jo*, it began…

She dragged in a painful breath and closed her eyes a moment before forcing them open and reading the letter he'd written to her some time before he'd been killed.

Three times she read it, before setting it back on the table and stumbling to her feet. She had to clutch the back of the chair to steady herself.

Luc walked in, took one look at her and crossed the room in long strides, demanding, 'What the hell's the matter?' as he grabbed her by the upper arms and supported her. 'It's all right,' he said roughly, pulling her stiff body into his arms. 'Whatever it is, we can deal with—'

'I know why Tom made it a condition that we live together,' Jo interrupted, her voice shaking.

Luc held her away from him, grey eyes searching her face. Struggling for control, she thrust out a hand towards the papers on the table. 'Look.'

His expression hardened. She waited for him to respond, but he said nothing until he'd put her back into the chair. Only then did he pick up the letter and began to read it.

Jo watched until he looked up, his narrowed eyes so dark they were almost black. 'He is— was—your *father*.'

'Yes.' Nausea and a great sorrow gripped her. 'My mother came to Rotumea twenty-three— no, twenty-four years ago. After my father—'

she stopped abruptly, then resumed '—the man she thought was my father was killed.'

'How old was she?'

'Eighteen,' she said succinctly.

His frown deepened. 'Tom would have been thirty-five.' He paused, then said deliberately, 'It was just after my mother told him she could have no more children. I suppose it makes sense.'

Jo shivered. After another stark few moments he asked, 'Why didn't she realise she was pregnant with his child?'

She swallowed. In a voice so muted he could hardly hear her, she said, 'I th-think it must have been because she believed she was already pregnant with my father's...with Joseph Thompson's baby.' She hesitated and swallowed, but clearly couldn't go on.

A surge of compassion and another unfamiliar emotion overtook Luc. Mentally consigning both Tom and Joanna's mother to some cold, dark region of outer space, he said, 'It must have been that. Otherwise—'

He stopped abruptly. He'd already made one huge mistake about Joanna; he wasn't going to compound his cynical mistake by saying that her mother would no doubt have asked for financial support if she'd realised the child she carried was Tom's.

In that steady, expressionless tone she said, 'She was engaged to him—to Joseph Thompson. They were going to get married, only he was killed in a road accident. Every Sunday we used to visit his grave and leave flowers on it. She loved him and missed him until the end of her life. I was named after him.'

Luc frowned. 'How could she have made such a mistake?'

'I don't know.' She shook her head, then said, 'But it's not possible to know the exact moment of conception.' Bright patches of colour flaked her high cheekbones. 'And there was only a week...'

Her voice trailed away as Luc nodded. Her mother's lover had died a week before she came to Rotumea; shortly after that, according to Tom, an attempt by him to comfort her had ended in his bed. If she already had cause to believe she might be pregnant it had probably never occurred to her that she carried Tom's child.

Tom's only child.

He asked, 'Are you all right?'

And thought disgustedly that of all the stupid things to ask, that was probably the most stupid. All right? How could she be *all right*? Everything she'd ever thought or believed about her family—the foundations of her life—had been turned upside down. No dead young father, her conception an accident known to no one, not even her mother.

'I'm OK,' she said automatically.

He scanned her white face. 'You don't look at all OK. In fact, you look as though you're going to faint.'

Her head came up and some fugitive colour stole through her white face. In a much stronger voice she said, 'I've never fainted in my life.'

'Nobody would blame you for starting now,' he said curtly, and turned away to get her a glass of water and put on the electric jug. She needed some stimulant—coffee would probably be best. He'd put some whisky in it and make her drink it.

Actually, he admitted grimly, he could do with a stiff whisky himself...

He looked across the room. 'Where did you find these papers?'

Limply she told him.

His eyes on the electric jug, he said, 'It appears that when you were a child Tom had no suspicion you might be his.'

'So he says...said.'

'But when you arrived here to look after your aunt he realised you not only *looked* like his mother—you sounded like her, have hair the same colour and texture.'

'Yes,' she said again numbly.

'Hence the DNA sample.' He waited, and when she said nothing he elaborated, 'It would have been easy enough to get one with you living in the house.'

'I suppose so,' she said, still in that flat, stunned voice.

Luc paused. 'Did you notice any change in his attitude to you?'

'No.' She thought for a moment, then said slowly, 'Actually, yes. I suppose I did.'

'In what way?' Luc demanded.

She searched for words. 'He talked to me about his family, about how he'd got to be the man he was—all sorts of things. I just thought he was lonely.' She pressed a clenched fist to her heart, then forced it away, staring at her fingers with a look that summoned another unfamiliar emotion in Luc. 'He was really helpful when I thought of starting my business—made me do a proper business plan, discussed it with me. He invited friends of his who came to the resort to dinner—people he respected—introduced me to them...'

Her voice trailed away.

Recalling his own scathing refusal to believe

anything she'd said about her relationship with Tom, Luc said bleakly, 'He did you few favours there—most of them are sure you were his mistress.'

She fired up. 'Then they must be totally lacking in any sort of empathy or understanding. He behaved like an uncle.' Again her voice thickened as she fought for composure. Taking a deep breath, she finished, 'Or a f-father.'

She dragged her gaze away from the letter to look back at him. 'But why keep it a secret? And why did Tom set up this whole situation?' She gestured wildly, encompassing the room and Luc.

'Tom trusted no one,' Luc told her uncompromisingly. 'Once he'd got this report, he wanted you to stay in Rotumea so he could find out what sort of person you are.'

She said numbly, 'It just seems…outrageous. Everything he's done. He was *testing* me?'

'Of course.' Luc paused, scanning her white face. That unusual compassion twisted his heart. She'd had enough.

But he owed her the truth—something Tom hadn't given her until too late.

He said, 'He was let down badly by his first wife. My mother married him because he was rich and was prepared to set up her family in the style they'd been accustomed to before they'd wasted their inheritance. After I was born she'd been told it was unlikely she'd have any more children, but she didn't tell Tom—she hoped the diagnosis was wrong. And I took Henderson's away from him. Why should he trust you?'

Jo was silent for a moment, then said quietly, 'I suppose I understand. At least we had that time together.'

Squaring her shoulders, she looked him in the eyes and said bluntly, 'I just thought he was lonely and bored. You'd taken over the enterprise he'd spent his life building, so it amused him to dabble in something as tiny as mine.' She paused, then decided to say it anyway. 'And it appeared you didn't care much about him.'

'I cared a lot,' he said curtly, adding in a level voice, 'but I also understood his desire to lick his wounds. Rotumea was his bolthole and his refuge. I'm sure he enjoyed helping you set up your business, and I'm equally sure he was pleased—and proud—to discover that his only child had something of his entrepreneurial spirit.'

'Just as he was proud of your ability,' she said, not quite knowing why.

Luc shrugged. 'I doubt that he ever thought of me as a son.'

Something about his tone caught her attention,

although her swift glance found no regret in his expression. A sharp pang of probably unnecessary sympathy persuaded Jo into an impulsive reply. 'He always spoke of you with pride and affection.'

'You don't have to sugar-coat his attitude,' he said with crisp disbelief.

Her head came up. 'I'm not. I don't lie. He certainly didn't like being dumped, but he was quite proud at how efficiently it was done, without weakening the business or lowering its value in the marketplace.'

Luc gave an ironic smile. 'Yes, that would be Tom.'

She shivered. 'He knew for almost two years that he was my father. It seems such a waste. We could have been a…a family.'

It hurt that he hadn't wanted that. After all, families accepted each other as they were—without testing them.

Or was that a stupidly sentimental view?

Not without sympathy, Luc said, 'He wouldn't have been Tom if he hadn't checked you out thoroughly.'

'But he *knew* me,' she protested, trying to contain her pain. 'I used to come to Rotumea at least once a year for the holidays. Quite often he was here. In a way, he watched me grow up.'

'He knew you as a child.' He shrugged. 'A woman is an entirely different thing.'

'Why didn't he trust women?' she asked directly.

After a few taut moments Luc answered, a trace of reluctance colouring his voice. 'His first wife enjoyed the money he was making, but resented the time it took—time away from her. A few years into the marriage, when he'd overstretched himself and was skating very close to bankruptcy, she left him for his biggest competitor.'

Jo thought that over before saying, 'So he had one bad experience with a woman and that turned him sour on all our sex?'

Luc shrugged and poured water into the coffee pot before saying, 'There would have been other experiences, I imagine. Rich men are targets for a certain type of person. Which was possibly why he chose my mother—a practical, unsentimental Frenchwoman who married him for his money.'

This seemed to be Jo's day to ask questions. Why not an impertinent one? He could only give her that steely look and refuse to answer. 'And what did she bring to the marriage?'

Then immediately wished she'd kept quiet. It

was too personal—something she had no right
to know.

However, instead of the stinging riposte she
expected, Luc said, 'This is guesswork—my
mother wasn't one to talk about her emotions.
She'd married once for love and that had been
a disaster. I imagine she agreed with her family
that her second marriage should be one of con-
venience. Tom was the ideal choice. And it was
happy enough.' His mouth twisted. 'Much happier than many I've seen that began with high
romance, only to disintegrate into chaos.'

Startled by this unexpected forthrightness, Jo
realised she and Luc did have something in common, after all—mothers who'd used their beauty
to secure a future for their children.

Luc went on, 'Their marriage was one of
equals; as her husband, he was introduced into
circles that boosted his career, and in return he
supported her—and me—in the style she believed was her due. He practically rebuilt the
chateau for her, and made sure she never wanted
for anything again.'

And possibly she'd hoped Tom would be satisfied with Luc as a substitute son.

How had that affected Luc? A quick glance
gleaned no information from his expression.

From what he'd said, she suspected he had his mother's very practical attitude to marriage.

He said levelly, 'Tom would have been pleased when he found out you were his daughter. But even then, he'd have wanted to be sure he could trust you with that knowledge.'

At Jo's soft, angry sound, Luc shrugged. 'The prospect of acquiring large amounts of money often changes people, bringing out the worst in them.'

She nodded, accepting the coffee he handed her. She'd read enough to know that was true.

Luc went on, 'He'd have planned to tell you in his own good time, but that bloody coconut robbed him of the opportunity.'

Tears clogging her voice, she said, 'He was so fit, he looked after himself, he ate well—he thought he'd live for ever.'

'He was sure he had all bases covered,' Luc agreed. He was watching her, his brows drawn together. 'You really were fond of him, weren't you?'

'Yes.' She blinked ferociously and steadied her voice. 'It's odd, isn't it? He was a father to you, and a sort of father to me, but he never knew what it was like to be a real father.' She glanced up with a smile that trembled. 'I suppose that makes us sort of siblings.'

'Like hell it does!' Luc took a step towards her, then stopped.

Jo's breath blocked her throat, something dying inside her as she watched him reimpose control. He said between his teeth, 'We share an affection for a man, that's all. And now we have to work out what to do about this situation.'

His words killed the hope she'd kept locked in her heart—a weak and feeble hope she'd refused to face.

Because facing it meant she'd have to accept something else—that her feelings for Luc went far deeper than mere lust.

'I know,' she said huskily.

He looked down at his clenched fists as though he'd never seen them before. 'First,' he stated, his voice showing no emotion, 'we have to see out the six months Tom stipulated.'

She opened her mouth, then closed it again. He was right. They had to do that. But at what cost to her? Luc wanted her—he'd admitted that. But somehow, without realising it, she'd grown to crave more than the passionate sating of desire. And one glance at his stony expression told her that even without the barrier of his beliefs about her relationship with Tom, Luc was not going to surrender to what he probably saw as a temporary passion.

The months ahead stretched out like a prison sentence.

'I suppose so,' she said quietly.

Luc looked down at her. 'Drink your coffee. The next thing we need to do is contact Tom's solicitor and get some advice about his revelations.'

She gave him a blank look. 'Why? He left me enough to live on for the rest of my life.'

'As his daughter, you have a claim to his entire estate,' Luc said briefly.

The cup in her hand trembled so much she set it down on the saucer. 'I don't want it,' she said, snapping each word out. 'I do *not* want anything more than he left me. I don't need it. If I end up with a fortune it will be one of my own making, not his. I will not contest the will.'

Luc looked at her, his mouth curving in a smile that held no hint of humour. 'Oh, yes,' he said levelly. 'You're his daughter, all right.'

And felt a coldly searing shame. Tom's silence and his own cynicism had made him angry and suspicious, even as he'd reluctantly come to admire her. *Admire?* He watched her get up, his gut tightening. There was a lot to admire about Joanna Forman, but that was too simple a word. His emotions were complex, warring with each other.

But he had time to assess them…

* * *

During the following weeks Jo sensed a subtle easing of Luc's aloofness. Slowly, carefully, without discussion, they negotiated a system of living together. She relished his dry sense of humour, and found herself eagerly driving home each afternoon to match wits with him. His keen intelligence intrigued her too much. And she enjoyed the rare moments when his spoken English revealed his French heritage.

However the tension was still there—ignored, controlled, but never entirely repressed. Luc had told her he felt nothing but lust for her, and she was too proud to be used.

So she warned herself to be satisfied that they were tentatively approaching something like acceptance of the situation.

The social life she instituted for them helped. The island chiefs and their wives were eager to meet Luc and, a little to her surprise, he seemed to enjoy being introduced to them.

'For a man who knows little of Pacific customs, you're proving very adaptable,' she said one evening, waving their last guests goodbye.

Luc gave her an ironic look. 'Protocol exists everywhere,' he observed negligently. 'Anyone with any common sense finds out what the prevailing customs and usages are before they travel. And these people are forgiving.'

And he made her laugh with a story of his naivety when he'd made his first trip to China, finishing by saying, 'They were charmingly polite about every mistake I made, and after that I vowed I wasn't going to be so stupid again.'

Perhaps it was the pleasant evening they'd had, or perhaps the eternal beauty of the stars overhead, jewelling the velvet sky with their ancient patterns, that persuaded Jo to ask something she'd often wondered about.

She said, 'Did you manage to deal satisfactorily with the mess you were handling while we were in Auckland?'

A certain grimness in his expression made her add hastily, 'If you can't talk about it, forget about it.'

His shoulders lifted briefly. 'I trust your discretion.'

Which startled her as well as gave her a suspicious frisson of pleasure.

Deliberately, Luc said, 'One of the executives there embezzled over a hundred thousand dollars.'

Shocked, she said, 'What was it—gambling?'

'That would have been easy to deal with. Her child—her oldest son—developed a rare form of cancer. She found that a highly experimental treatment was on offer in America. She didn't have the money to pay for it, and couldn't get it anywhere, so she took it.'

Jo frowned. 'What happened to the boy?'

'He died,' he said shortly.

'Oh, that's so sad.'

'Yes. No happy endings.'

Glancing up at the autocratic profile etched against that radiant sky, Jo decided not to ask how he'd dealt with the situation.

However, he said, 'We came to a decision that satisfied everyone.'

Including the poor woman who'd lost her son?

He went on, 'She's still working for us—under stringent supervision—and will pay back the money.'

And that did surprise her. When she remained silent he gave a swift, sardonic smile. 'You thought I'd sack her? Prosecute her?'

'Well, actually, yes,' she admitted.

'I do have the occasional moment of compassion,' he said smoothly. 'She is an excellent executive, and she's paid a heavy enough price—her marriage broke up over her actions and the strain of their son's illness.'

If she hadn't known that nothing cracked that granite façade he presented to the world, she thought a little wistfully, she might have thought her comment had struck a nerve.

Quite often they dined at the resort, occasionally with friends or business associates of Luc's who'd flown in. To Jo's surprise, she liked his friends. His easy companionship with them led to some wistful moments. Slowly, guiltily, she realised she wanted more—much, much more— from Luc than friendship.

Each day his controlled courtesy grated more, pulling taut a set of nerves she hadn't known she possessed. Adding to her stress was the slow progress of the Council of chiefs on making any decision. They had accepted Tom's document, but Meru's cousin remained infuriatingly silent about any deliberations.

Between fear for the future of her business and her growing feelings for Luc, Jo endured long nights when she turned restlessly in her bed and wondered whether he too was awake—so close and yet so distant from her.

Almost certainly not…

It was a relief when, after a telephone call, Luc informed her he had to go to China for a meeting. 'We'll leave tomorrow and be away for five days.'

'I can't come.'

'Why not? I think you'd enjoy Shanghai, and contacts there should be valuable.'

'I can't leave Rotumea because any day now—I hope—I'll learn whether I still have a business,' she told him.

'What?' He frowned and asked curtly, 'What's going on?'

When she'd explained what was happening, his frown deepened. 'All right, obviously you have to be here for that.' He paused. 'Shall I stay?'

'No,' she said, touched by his thoughtfulness. 'It may not be decided yet. They hoped to have a consensus by now, but a couple of expatriate chiefs arrived from New Zealand yesterday, and they'll probably bring the wishes of the Rotumean community there to be considered.'

But there was no decision for several days. 'Something has happened,' Meru told her. 'I don't know what it is, but it means they cannot come to a decision yet.' She paused, then said quietly, 'I think you are going to lose, Jo. They will be very sorry, but of course they have to think of everyone, not just you. And this firm is promising big things—they have a very good ecological reputation, you know, and they are prepared to work with the Council to make sure the island is not changed in any way.'

'I know,' Jo said huskily. 'It's all right, don't worry.'

On the day Luc was due back, Jo woke late, slitting her eyes against the bright morning light. He'd been away less than a week, yet she'd missed him. How she'd missed him! His absence was an aching gap in her life, a silent emptiness that echoed through the days and haunted her sleep at night.

For the past two months she'd been continually tense, struggling to contain a need that grew ever stronger, engraving itself on her heart so deeply she'd never be able to erase it.

She gritted her teeth. She could cope; she had to cope. In a few months they'd have fulfilled the conditions of Tom's will, and could pick up their lives again. And she'd be spared the pain of seeing Luc ever again.

A gull called from outside, its shrill screech drowned out by the alarm siren of the blackbird in the garden. Taken by surprise, she hurled back the sheet and leapt out. That bird was a drama queen, but something or someone was out there, and today Luc was coming home—no, she corrected, he was coming *back*. Rotumea wasn't his home, never would be. Just as it wasn't hers.

Yet excitement exploded through her, a starburst of foolish anticipation doomed to be frustrated.

She grabbed the first thing to hand—a sarong slung over the back of a chair—but had only wound it halfway round her when she heard a car door slam. She snatched up a hairbrush, dragging it through her tangled locks, then took a deep breath and walked out onto the terrace, stopping after the first step. Her heart contracted.

Watching the blackbird as it peered nervously through the screen of hibiscus blossoms, Luc stood against a screen of bold magenta bougainvillea. A half-smile curled his mouth. Her heart began to beat rapidly. He was so...so *magnificent*, hair gleaming in the golden light, his natural tan deepened by the tropical sun.

And she loved him.

CHAPTER TEN

THE REALISATION HIT Jo with the force of a blow, shocking her into immobility. Panicking, she heard herself drag in a jagged breath. It wasn't possible. She didn't know Luc well enough to take that final step. He'd shown himself to be judgemental and inflexible and autocratic and intolerant and...her mind ran out of adjectives.

But not recently, she thought despairingly. And then Luc turned, his face hardening when he saw her. Suddenly aware of her scanty sarong, she shot backwards into the shade of the terrace.

In a voice that sounded as though he'd been goaded beyond bearing, he demanded harshly, 'Damn you, Joanna, why can't you be dressed and ready to go to work?'

The words whirling around her mind, she blinked.

He headed purposefully towards her, stopping only a few inches away. Eyes widening,

she stared up into his face. He looked as though
it had been a hard sojourn in Shanghai. His arrogant bone structure was more prominent, but
the grey eyes were hot and urgent, and when he
made an odd sound deep in his throat and pulled
her into his arms she didn't resist, melting into
him with a shaky sigh of relief.

'What happened with the Council of chiefs?'
he demanded.

She tried to pull away, but his arms tightened.
'They're still talking.'

His face hardened. 'How long do they need?'

He was holding her so close she could feel the
stirring of his body, the hard shifting and flexion of muscles as though he clamped some tight
control on them.

'Luc,' she said fiercely into his chest, 'let *go*.'

'You want this—don't lie to me, Joanna, I see
it in your eyes every time you look at me.' His
voice was rough and harsh, and the pressure of
his arms around her didn't slacken.

'I didn't mean let *me* go,' she said indig-
nantly, jerking her head upwards to glare at him.
'*You*—I meant let yourself go.'

He stared at her as though she were mad,
then startled her by emitting a short, unamused
laugh. 'Very well, then—but only if it's mutual.'

Jo's heart missed a beat. 'You've just said you know it is.'

His eyes narrowed. 'The passion is mutual—how about the surrender?'

For a moment she hesitated, but only for a moment. 'Of course it is,' she said fiercely.

He bent his head. But instead of the fierce hunger she expected, his kiss was soft and tantalising, a slow sweet pressure that sent her pulse soaring. Enraptured, she returned it, letting instinct take over to openly reveal the love that had flowered within her so unexpectedly.

He lifted his head and surveyed her with an intent, almost silver scrutiny. 'Enough?' he asked.

'No.' A sudden thought struck her. 'Unless you're tired,' she added heroically, every cell in her body objecting to such restraint.

Something moved in his eyes. 'Not *too* tired,' he said in that thick, hard voice, and startled her by lifting her as though she were a child and shouldering through the doorway.

He carried her into her bedroom, standing for a few seconds to survey the tangled sheets on the bed before easing her onto her feet.

This time his kiss was different, much more carnal. Jo's blazing response shocked her—her reckless, overt need was both delicious and intoxicating, singing through her body like a siren's lure.

When he lifted his head and held her a half-step away her sarong fell to the floor, a puddle of coral and peach and blue-violet, leaving her only in her narrow bikini briefs.

Luc's hands tightened on her shoulders, then relaxed.

Eyes kindling, he said, 'You're beautiful. But you know that. And I want you—you've known that too, ever since we first set eyes on each other. And at the moment I don't give a damn for all the reasons we shouldn't be doing this.'

Jo had never felt so sensuous, so at home. The soft sea breeze caressed her skin, lifting the ends of her hair around her face, and Luc looked at her as though she was all he'd ever desired. She didn't know what to do, what to say.

So she let her expression tell him that a desperate need raced through her like some headstrong tide, carrying her further and further away from safety.

Nothing else but this moment, this sensation, made sense to her.

'Neither do I,' she said honestly, and reached out to touch his shoulder, tracing the hard swell of a muscle with a light, sensuous finger.

He tensed as though she'd hit him, then gave

a low, triumphant laugh and yanked his shirt over his head, before stripping off the rest of his clothes.

Her low, feral murmur took her by surprise. It surprised him too, but he smiled and lifted a hand that shook slightly, reaching for her again, easing her against him as though she was precious to him.

Sighing with voluptuous pleasure, Jo relaxed against him, shamelessly letting him support her.

When his lips met hers rational thought fled, banishing all foreboding as she surrendered to the magic of her stimulated senses, the pressure of Luc's mouth as he explored hers, the erotic slide of heated skin against skin...

He lifted her again and set her down on the bed, sprawled across the sheets she'd left only a few minutes previously. He didn't join her; instead he stood like some pagan conqueror gazing down at one of the spoils of war.

In his face she read a fierce appetite that matched hers, roused it further and took her higher than she'd ever been. Without thinking, she held out her arms to him.

He didn't move.

Surely he wasn't going to call a halt now...

Quickly, before she could think better of it, she blurted, 'I'm taking the Pill.'

Luc's smile was taut and fierce. 'And I've got protection.'

Her heart soared as he came down beside her in a movement that lacked a little of his usual litheness, and slid his arms around her as though he too had been craving this moment, dreaming of it night and day, desired it like a man lost in the desert longed for water.

He bent his head, but didn't take her hungry mouth. Disappointment ached through her, only to disappear when he dropped a sinuous line of kisses from the corner of her mouth to the pulse in her throat.

'You taste like honey and cream,' he said against its frantic throbbing. 'Sweet and rich, with a tang.'

Shudders of exquisite pleasure shivered along her nerves, as he found the lobe of her ear and bit it gently.

With the pathetic remains of her willpower, Jo held back a gasp, sighing languorously when he transferred to the juncture of her neck and shoulder, biting again so gently she could barely feel it. More pleasure shimmered through her.

'I didn't know—' she breathed into his throat,

her voice dying when he bit again, applying slightly more pressure.

'What didn't you know?' His voice was low and raw, as though he was holding himself in rigid restraint.

'That it—that anything could feel so good,' she whispered.

'Here?' Another sensuous nip sent more excitement seething through her.

'Yes,' she croaked, and turned her head to do the same to him, her hand over his heart.

She felt it leap beneath her palm, felt the swift tension in his muscles. A sense of power, of communion, of a subtle forging of bonds, surged through her when he slid a hand down to cup her breast, the lean fingers gentle yet assured as they stroked the tip into a taut little peak.

A groan ripped from her throat and her body tightened, driven by an urgency that brooked no disappointment.

'Ah, yes, you like that,' he breathed, and bent his head to kiss the spot, then took it into his mouth.

'Luc…' His name emerged as a long, shuddering sigh.

He lifted his head and watched her tremble with something so close to rapture it made her need even more keen, piercing her with a demand she couldn't articulate.

His hand slid further down, traced the narrow curve of her waist, moved past her hip and found the slick, heated folds at the juncture of her thighs.

'Yes,' he said, and came over her, testing her gently until she seized him by the shoulders and pulled him down and into her, drugged by a sensuous craving that insisted on satisfaction.

Her boldness cracked his iron control. A rough, feral noise erupted from deep in his throat and he thrust, deep and ever deeper, until at last the mounting wave of ecstasy broke over her, carrying her so far beyond rapture she thought her heart would break its bounds.

Even as the wave crested and ebbed he flung his head back, muscles coiled and flowing while he took his fill of her, finally easing down with her into a sated serenity punctuated only by the heavy beating of her heart against his.

Jo had never felt such sweet sorrow at the end of exhilaration, yet with it came a powerful contentment and peace, as though the experience had gone beyond the physical and was transformed into something spiritual.

For her, her mind told her drowsily. Not for Luc...

Right then, she didn't care. It was enough to hold him while their pulses synchronised to a steady regular beat, to savour his weight on her, his long muscles lax, his head on the pillow beside her.

But too soon he said, 'I'm far too heavy for you,' and before she could tighten her arms around him he turned onto his side and pulled her against him with her head on his shoulder.

No, you're not...I think I might have been born for this. Another thing she didn't dare say aloud.

So she made an indeterminate noise, and they lay together until he said, 'If I don't move soon I might go to sleep.'

Love and concern for him forced her to remember he'd flown in from China.

'Didn't you sleep on the plane?' she asked.

He paused, then gave a short laugh. 'Not much.' He released her and swung himself off the bed. For a moment he looked down at her, grey eyes narrowed and unreadable, before turning away and beginning to pull on his clothes.

Jo lay for a few seconds, wondering what to say, where to go from here. Before she'd made up her mind, he picked up her sarong and tossed it to her.

'Too tempting,' he said harshly.

Fumbling, she draped the cloth around her,

feeling oddly empty, only to have to stand up and arrange it.

Fully dressed, Luc asked dryly, 'What happened to the businesswoman who raced off to work at the crack of dawn every day?'

Her whole world had changed, yet nothing had; they were back to fencing with each other. Perhaps the foils had been blunted a little, but they were still sharp.

Steadying her voice, she said, 'She got waylaid,' and then blushed. 'I'll head off in half an hour or so,' she said quickly. 'You'll be able to sleep then if you want to.'

'Jo,' he said quietly.

Desperately clinging to the remnants of her dignity, she faced him. 'What?'

He paused, scrutinising her face before saying, 'I thought I had enough strength of mind to resist you. I was wrong. Are you all right?'

Pride provided the answer. She even managed a smile. 'Of course,' she told him brightly. 'You don't have to be told you're a magnificent lover, surely?'

And was bemused by the tinge of colour along his autocratic cheekbones when he said, 'I'm glad you think so. It was…special for me too. And we need to talk once you get home again.' He turned and left the room.

His tone had been courteous enough, but an undernote to his words stayed with her. It hadn't been contempt, yet it left her feeling oddly disassociated and uneasy, and she spent too much time that morning at work wondering about it when she should have been marshalling her argument for continuing her contract with the Council of chiefs.

It was a relief when Meru knocked on her door, even though the older woman looked worried. 'Jo, something's happened,' she said.

Jo's heart skipped a beat. She'd believed she was ready for what was probably going to be a refusal, but the worry that clawed at her was fierce and devastating. 'Do you think the decision will be made today? Has your cousin any idea which way the chiefs might be going?'

Meru sighed and sat down. 'Yes. But something unexpected has happened.'

'What?' The single word snapped out.

'There has been another offer.'

Whatever she'd expected, it wasn't this. 'From whom?' she asked blankly.

'I don't know, but it raises the first offer. I think we are going to lose, Jo.'

Jo reined in her shocked dismay. 'In that case, get your cousin to persuade the Council to sign a written contract—one made out by powerful lawyers who know the island. One that stipulates all of our employees' jobs will be safe.'

'Yes.' Meru looked anxiously at her. 'Jo, what will you do?'

Jo swallowed a lump in her throat. 'I'll set up another business—in New Zealand, probably.'

Meru's eyes filled with tears. 'We'll miss you,' she said, and came across and hugged her hard.

When she'd gone Jo sat for long moments, staring blindly at the computer screen.

Everything had been pushed off balance, all the foundations of her life revealed to be shaky. The knowledge that she was Tom's daughter had begun the process...

No, she thought, determined to face facts. Meeting Luc had started it. She'd started by disliking him as she fought that fierce physical attraction, then reluctantly learned to respect him. Falling in love had stolen up on her, ambushed her heart. *Making* love with him had set the seal on her change of emotions, and it had been— life-changing.

The end of all her dreams and plans for her business was life-changing too, she thought wearily, only in an entirely different way. Before she'd met Luc she'd have been completely devastated by the loss of her business, but that unexpected, newfound love had changed her.

What now?

Love battled with desire, fought caution, resisted everything that urged—begged, demanded, *insisted*—she yield to it.

She got to her feet and walked across to the window, staring out across the rustling feathery tops of the coconut palms. The faint evocative perfume of gardenia mingled with petrol fumes and the ever-present salty tang. Heat hit her like a blow. Closing her eyes, she wrestled her way to the hardest decision she'd ever made—much more difficult than choosing to care for her mother in the face of Kyle's threat to walk out on their relationship.

Did she have the courage to take the chance that Luc might learn to love her?

It didn't seem likely. All his lovers had been beautiful, yet the relationships had died. Did he even believe in love—the unconditional sort her mother had known, a love that lasted a lifetime? Because only that would satisfy her.

It didn't seem likely.

And she couldn't—wouldn't—cope with emotionless sex that meant nothing more than the satisfaction of carnal needs. Loving Luc as she did, such a surrender would kill something vital, something honest and basic in her.

So she'd tell Luc there would be no more rapturous moments in his arms...

Her hands clenched on the windowsill.

Glimpsing paradise only to be forced to repudiate it would be like enduring hell, but she had to do it.

At least Luc wasn't at home when she reached the house. Shaking inwardly, Jo went inside and showered, turning off the water to hear a car coming towards the house. Luc, she thought, her heart going suddenly into overdrive. She dragged on a long loose shift before forcing herself to walk sedately outside.

That foolish wild anticipation abruptly died when she opened the door to Sean Harvey. He surveyed her with the insolent half-smile that had become his usual greeting for her.

'Hi, gorgeous,' he said, eyeing her up and down. 'How are things going?'

'Fine, thank you,' she said without warmth.

'I hear you've had some good luck.'

Uneasy under his stare, she asked, 'Really?'

Then remembered with relief that she'd been interviewed by the local newspaper a few days previously, and had mentioned that the latest range of skincare creams had been accepted into one of New York's most prestigious stores.

'Yep.' He never took his eyes off her. 'Word is that you're actually Tom Henderson's daughter.'

She felt the colour drain from her face. 'Really?' she said again, buying time. 'And where did you hear that?'

'Around,' he said casually. 'Is it true?'

She shrugged. 'My ancestry is no one's concern but mine.'

'So it is true,' he said, still watching her, his gaze as cold as a shark's. 'Why not admit it?'

'Why did you come here?'

He sneered, 'Could the secrecy have anything to do with your mother being a call girl? Was old Tom ashamed of you?'

'My mother was not a call girl,' she said sharply, despising him and so angry she had to stop and draw breath before she could say, 'Pity *your* mother didn't wash your mouth out with soap more often. I don't know why you're here, and you can leave right now.'

'What if I don't want to? After all, your lover's not here. You must be lonely, looking for a little warmth.'

She stepped back and slammed the door in his face, knowing it was flimsy protection. The house had few external walls.

At least the sound of a car engine meant Sean wasn't hanging around. Relief almost swamped her until she realised the vehicle was coming down the drive, not going away. The engine died, followed by a second's silence before she heard Luc's voice. His icy, ominous tone sent a shiver scudding down her spine.

Fingers shaking, she opened the door to see Sean trying to maintain his insolence in the face of Luc's anger. As she stepped out, Sean's hand clenched into a fist and he took a step towards Luc, lowering his head like a charging bull.

Shock ricocheted through her.

In a silky voice loaded with menace, Luc ordered, 'Don't try it.'

Intensely relieved, she saw Sean hesitate then drop his hands and step back.

'Sean's just going,' she said crisply.

Without looking at her, Luc ordered, 'On your way, then.'

Sean waited until he was in his car before he wound down the window and sneered, 'Not even you can put a stop to this, you know. Everyone on Rotumea knows.'

Gravel spurted from the wheels as the car surged forward, missing Luc by a foot, then shot down the drive.

Luc came to the door in a swift, noiseless rush, his expression controlled. 'What the hell was he doing here?' he demanded.

'He came to tell me he knows I'm Tom's daughter,' she told him shakily, furious with him. 'Luc, he tried to run you over! Why didn't you get out of the way?'

'I've outbluffed better players than him,' he said contemptuously. 'How did he find out?'

'I don't know, and I don't care.' She expelled pent-up air and steadied her voice. 'I don't know why he's being so...so *stupid*! We've never been anything more than friends—and not even that after the night he bailed me up at the resort.'

The night she'd met Luc. It seemed so long ago, as though she'd never lived before she met him...

He said now, 'I did tell you once that money has the power to change most people. Get used to it.'

'But *I* haven't changed!' She combated her fear and anger by banging a fist on the balustrade. 'I'm just the same person I was before!' And stopped, because of course she wasn't. She'd changed, but it had been love that did that, not money.

Luc took her elbow and steered her through the door. 'What did you tell him when he said he knew?'

'That my ancestry was no one's business

but mine.' She took in a deep breath of warm, flower-scented air and tried to compose herself.

'And you've not told anyone?'

'No.' But then she felt colour drain from her face.

'You did.' He sounded bored, as though it was only to be expected.

Realising she was clutching his sleeve, she dropped her hand and took a deep breath while she strode across to the kitchen. Defiantly she said, 'Yes. Lindy.' And shook her head. 'But Lindy wouldn't tell anyone—I asked her not to.'

'Not her husband?'

She hesitated. 'I don't think she'd tell him. I don't know.'

'Marriage changes people too. She might think you didn't mean him.'

His cynical intonation made her angry. 'Surely it doesn't matter? I didn't tell her about the condition in Tom's will.'

'It matters,' Luc said curtly. 'Brace yourself, because the media is on the way. A gossip columnist got in touch with me an hour ago.' He demanded abruptly, 'Have you seen your lawyer yet?'

Hands shaking, she opened the fridge and got out the iced water. 'No. I told you, I don't need to.'

Luc said something under his breath, and she

hurried on, 'It's nobody's business but mine who my parents were.'

'Agreed, except that as Tom's only child you have a moral claim to his estate.'

'I don't,' she said instantly, swinging around to fix him with a fierce glare. 'I don't want anything to do with it. I'll take what he left me, but no more. As for the press—well, they can say what they like. I'll stay here—they'll soon get bored in Rotumea.'

His gaze narrowed, then he shrugged. 'I'll get changed and then we'll talk.'

Ten minutes later, walking beside him along the beach, Jo tried to stifle a tenuous joy that could only be temporary.

Casually, Luc asked, 'Why don't you want anything more from Tom's estate?'

Jo stopped, watching a frigate bird soar and wheel in the sky. The sun dazzled her eyes and the familiar roar of the waves on the coral reef was no comfort.

She tried to organise her objection into words that made sense, finally saying, 'If he'd told me—if we'd been able to relate to each other, forge some sort of family feeling—I might feel differently.'

'I can understand that, but you told me that he treated you like an uncle—or a father.'

Surprised that he'd remembered, she said, 'He did, but…I never felt that we were family, the way it was with my mother and Aunt Luisa. If I'd known—if he'd told me—I might feel I have some further claim on his estate, even though he left me more than enough. But then, if he'd wanted me to have anything more than what he left me in his will he'd have seen to it. He didn't.'

He stopped and looked down at her, grey eyes hooded. 'He probably intended to before that damned hurricane.'

'In the Pacific they're called cyclones,' she said bleakly. 'And you don't know what he'd have done.'

She tried again to make him understand. 'Luc, I don't want anything more. I was shocked enough to get what I did. You deserve to head Henderson's. I think he knew that, even if he was angry with you for taking his place.'

Hoping she'd said enough to convince him, she met his piercing gaze staunchly. 'I don't know what lever Tom used to force you to obey his condition, but he had no right to do it.'

'His lever,' he told her deliberately, 'is that you have the power to make my life a hell of a lot harder.'

'What?' For a moment she thought her heart had stopped beating. She'd had too many shocks this morning. This was something she couldn't—didn't want to—deal with.

The cold, controlled anger hardening his expression cut her breath short. Pulse thundering in her ears, she waited.

He said, 'At the end of six months you'll be asked by the solicitor how you feel about me. Your opinion decides whether or not I take full control of Tom's estate.' His face more arrogant than she'd ever seen it, he went on, 'It won't be the end of the world if you say I'm the biggest bastard you've ever come across—I'll get what I want eventually, but possibly not before considerable damage has been done to Henderson's. The shares will fall once shareholders hear you're his daughter.'

'Why?'

'They'll anticipate a legal battle for control.'

'So that's why...' Jo stopped, unable to continue. Now she knew why he'd relaxed his iron restraint enough to make love to her—because he wanted that power, that control over Tom's empire.

Sick to her soul with disillusion, she closed her eyes. Loving him was breaking her heart, but this—this was even worse.

'That's why I agreed to this farcical situation,' he said, each word clipped and cold and precise.

Whatever Tom had intended by his eccentric will, it couldn't be allowed to wreck Luc's career. But oh, how could he have used her with such calculated cynicism?

Pride forced her voice to remain steady. 'And after you'd vented your spleen for a few weeks by being as nasty as you could, did you decide that seducing me into some meaningless love-making would be the easiest route to my agreement?'

'Don't try to tell me that this morning meant nothing to you,' he said between his teeth. 'I was there, Joanna. I know how you look when we make love, and it wasn't *meaningless*.'

She stopped, and turned blindly back. *No*, she thought in anguish as his hand on her arm froze her into place. *No, don't try to persuade me with lies...*

He said, 'I made love to you because I couldn't stop myself. And because you wanted me as much as I wanted you. I wasn't capable of thinking beyond that—certainly not planning to seduce you.'

'Let me go,' she said thinly.

He paused, then let his hand fall. Jo set off towards the house, her thoughts in turmoil, her insides churning. He caught her up after a pace.

Dragging in a long silent breath, she said as

calmly as she could, 'You don't need to worry. I'll stay. When the six months are up I'll tell Mr Keller that you're the ideal person to take over Henderson Holdings.'

Luc examined her silently. She was pale and her voice was shaky, but she met his gaze without wavering.

'Tom's played with our lives enough,' she said dispassionately. 'I don't want to live by his rules any longer. From now on, I suggest we don't mention his name. And I'll try not to get in your way.'

What the hell did she mean by that? Luc suspected he knew. She was closing the door firmly on any further lovemaking. After a silent, furious epithet, he tried to convince himself it was sensible.

Hell, you've made a total hash of this.

Surprising himself, he realised he believed she'd keep her word once this damned probation period was over. Probably because she'd fought so hard for her small business—not for herself so much as for the people who worked for her.

Yet every fibre of his body was taut and angry, as though something infinitely precious had been taken from him. Sensible or not, he wanted her in his bed. Their lovemaking had been a wondrous thing, satisfying a need he hadn't known existed in him.

If he believed in love, he might even think he was halfway there.

It was going to be sheer hell keeping his distance. But he'd misjudged her so badly he owed her that.

'Right, it's a deal,' he said, and held out his hand.

After a moment's hesitation she put hers in his. Her grip was warm but soon loosened, and images of her almost shy caresses, of the heat of her body and her ecstasy in his arms flashed into his mind.

His treacherous body reacted immediately. He dropped her hand and took a pace backwards. 'That's settled, then,' he said, controlling a primitive urge to take her in his arms and comfort her. 'No more dancing to Tom's tune. But you do need to talk to a lawyer about this. Do you have one?'

Long lashes shielded those slumbrous green eyes, hiding her emotions from him. 'I use the local one,' she said. 'And I don't see any reason to consult a solicitor; if you can cope with the next few months, so can I, and then it will be over.'

And we can go our separate ways, her tone told him.

Luc set his jaw. 'Nevertheless, see the lawyer.' He glanced at his watch. 'Right now, I suggest we go to the resort and have lunch.'

The more people around them the better; at the resort he'd be able to subdue his fierce desire to pull her into him and kiss her into submission, before making love to her all afternoon.

The effort showing, she shrugged. 'I'll just snatch a sandwich here—I have to meet the chiefs this afternoon to hear the result of their interminable deliberations.'

He nodded. 'Good luck.'

In spite of everything, she thought almost bitterly as she turned away, it hurt that he didn't offer to accompany her. Moral support would have been welcome.

Joanna arrived back at the house well after the swift tropical twilight had darkened into a velvet night. Luc heard the sound of her car and half-turned in the shelter of one of the big trees by the beach. Immediately he forced himself to stay. He'd been trying to make sense of the decision he'd come to—and was failing.

Infuriatingly, his desire still warred with his intellect. Why had he been crazy enough to reveal the power she'd been given in Tom's will? It had been a huge, reckless gamble—yet it had been the right thing to do.

What he really wanted to know was the reason she'd given him her loyalty. Because that was what she'd done when she'd told him she'd stay on so that he could keep his position at Henderson's without the infighting that would be inevitable if he'd been deprived of it.

As though she knew where to find him, she walked swiftly down the path beneath the coconut palms. He waited until she was within a pace before asking, 'What was the decision?'

With a little cry she swivelled. 'Oh,' she said, exhaustion flattening her voice. 'I didn't see you.'

'I realised that.' His voice was dry.

Abruptly she told him, 'The Council decided not to take up the other offer.'

Silence stretched between them, tense with unspoken words, hidden emotions. Luc broke it. 'Good,' he said roughly. 'Jo, marry me.'

Stunned, Jo stared at him, her involuntary flash of incredulous joy evaporating as quickly as it had come. She drew a sharp breath and blurted, 'Don't be an idiot.'

But her voice broke. Desperately she hoped

he hadn't caught that moment of sheer elation. What on earth was he doing now?

He shrugged, his expression unreadable in the darkness. 'This is the first proposal I've ever made, so I'm probably making a total hash of it, but I'd hoped that by now you'd have realised I'm no idiot.'

'Luc, this is ridiculous.' It took every ounce of self-possession to ignore the splintering of her heart. 'You don't have to marry me to make sure I'll keep our deal.'

'That's not why I asked you,' he said roughly.

'Then why did you?' A spark of humiliation persuaded her to ask, 'Because the sex was good? I'm sure you've had just as good before.'

'You have every right to be bitter, but I did not make love with you to win you onto my side.'

She drew in a deep breath. 'I'm not into expedient marriages, I'm afraid, like your—' and stopped precipitately because she'd just about been unforgivably rude.

Of course he guessed what she'd been going to say. 'Like my mother? Her first one wasn't expedient—it was all lust and parental defiance. The second was certainly financially practical.' He didn't wait for an answer. 'I'm not offering anything like the bargain she made with Tom.'

Jo had to boost her faltering courage to ask, 'So what *are* you offering?'

And *why*? Because there could only be one *good* reason—love.

He paused for at least three heartbeats. 'Ours would be a marriage of equals.'

Sorely torn, Jo hesitated, then took the biggest gamble of her life. 'I must be like *my* mother. She loved Joseph until she died—his name was the last word she said. I think that's possibly why she chose the life she did. She was no call girl,' she added, Sean's contempt vivid in her mind. 'She was a model and, in spite of the gossip, her relationships were long and faithful.'

'So *tell* me,' Luc said in a voice she'd never heard before. He stepped out of the shadows and looked down at her, starlight emphasising the strong bones of his face. 'Tell me what you want.'

'I've just told you.' She dragged in another jagged breath and met fierce grey eyes, narrowed and demanding. 'I want to marry someone I love—without limits, without fear, with total commitment and honesty.'

He said between his teeth, 'When we made love you gave me everything, without limits.'

'Desire isn't love,' she said sadly.

'I think that's what I've been trying to tell

you.' He didn't move and his gaze never left her face. 'I've been attracted to women, lusted after some, made love to a few. Love is not a word I've ever used. Jo, do you feel anything more for me than passion?'

'I…I…' She struggled for words, then surrendered to the hard command of his expression. 'Of course I do. I love you. But that's not…'

When she stopped, he waited a few seconds before saying levelly, 'Go on.'

'That's not what you want to hear, is it?'

Incredulously, she saw his hands clench by his sides. 'I can't tell you I love you because I don't know what that is. I've had no experience of it. I *can* tell you that in spite of all I believed about you, I wanted you from the moment I saw you. It tore me apart. And as I got to know you I learned—with immense reluctance—to admire you. You're staunch and fearless and loyal, you work for what you believe in. You forced me to accept that you were not the woman I believed you to be.'

Eyes still holding hers, he shook his head. 'I'll admit I toyed with the idea of seducing you to make sure you gave me a good recommendation. I wanted to despise you for selling yourself to Tom, yet I couldn't reconcile my prejudice with the woman who spoke of him with such affection—a woman who'd cared for her sick mother and aunt, the woman whose main worry when her business was threatened was the welfare of her workers. Every day I saw some new instance of your spirit and your honesty, until I gave up looking for the wicked gold digger. If this is not love, trust me, it's a damned good substitute.'

'But will it last?' she asked quietly, unable to articulate the inchoate mass of doubts and fears that swirled through her.

'As long as I live.'

It sounded like a vow.

Jo looked at him and tried to speak but the words died in her throat and tears sprang to her eyes.

'Don't *do* that!' he ordered roughly. 'Joanna, marry me and I swear you'll never regret it.'

A wild response shuddered through her, insisting that she take this chance, and surrender without reservations.

But all she could say was, 'All right,' followed by a yelp of shock when he swooped and lifted her, and held her in a grip so tight she gasped for breath.

'Oh, *hell*,' he said remorsefully, and put her down and kissed her. After a while he looked around and said in a low, intense voice, 'Much as I'd like to make love to you here, there's a canoe with three fishermen in it not more than fifty metres out in the lagoon. Come back to the house with me.'

Laughing, tears still weirdly falling, she took the hand he held out and turned back to the house with him. 'It will be all over the island within two hours,' she gasped.

'Do you mind?'

'Not a bit.'

He lifted her hand and kissed the palm, then tucked it into the crook of his arm. 'There's nothing we can do about the media. And there will be innuendos—that I've married you only because you're Tom's daughter.'

She pulled a face. 'So, who cares?'

Luc grinned and hugged her. 'His will won't be accessible to the public until it's probated, which will give us some time to brace ourselves. Although, if I know Tom, that provision will never be available.'

'Do you think he had some idea of this? Of us?'

He looked down at her. 'I don't know, but I wouldn't be in the least surprised. Would you?'

Jo shook her head. 'No, not surprised at all,' she said slowly. 'Luc, do you mind if we get married here?'

'When?'

She laughed, feeling an enormous lightness and freedom and—yes, relief, as though everything had come together for her and Luc. He hadn't said he loved her—and she valued his honesty. One day, she thought with complete trust, one day he'd say it and she'd value the words even more because he'd wanted to be certain.

'In three weeks,' she said demurely. 'That's how long it takes here in paradise.'

They were married on the beach in front of the house, with friends around them. Jo wore a long floating sarong—cream silk appliquéd with pale gold hibiscus flowers made by the local grandmothers during their sewing meetings. Frangipani flowers the same colour were tucked into her hair, and her sandals were jewelled with the glittering beads that adorned her bolero jacket. She carried a spray of the precious gardenia from the island, its scent floating clear and sensuous in the sultry air.

The reception was a glorious mixture of Polynesian, European and French customs, as were the guests. Lindy was maid of honour, still mortified that a workmate had overheard her tell her husband that her best friend, Jo Forman, was Tom Henderson's—yes, *that* Tom Henderson—*daughter…*

It was a noisy, touching ceremony, the church choir adding their superb harmonies to the gentle hush of the waves on the beach. Jo blinked back tears several times, her hand firmly held by her new husband as they were congratulated by Luc's friends—some with faces seen often in the news—and hers, by her workers and several old school friends.

'Meru told me something today that made me realise how very lucky I am,' she told her husband, when the music and dancing had died away, and the guests had trooped off, leaving the beach empty once more. The sun had long set, and a golden lover's moon hung close to the tops of the coconut palms, casting its enchantment over the island and the sea.

Luc cocked a brow. 'What?'

'She told me that the reason the Council of chiefs didn't sell the rights to their plants was because they were made a better offer by someone else.'

He looked bored. 'Doesn't sound likely,' he said dismissively.

An upwelling of something close to pure delight tinged her smile with magic. 'It doesn't, does it? Would you like to know who made that offer?'

He shrugged. 'None of my business.'

'As it happens, I haven't been told,' she told him. 'Neither was Meru. It's a deep, dark secret, but she said she was pretty certain you know.'

He looked down at her, eyes silver in the moonlight, and laughed. 'I suppose you want me to tell you who it is?'

His body tightened when she sent him a glance that was both demure and mischievous. 'I don't think you should make it too easy for me to find out.'

Luc's grin widened. 'How good are your powers of persuasion?'

'I've never extended them before, but I bet they'll do the trick.'

'I like your style,' he said, and turned her into his arms and looked down at her. 'In fact, I like everything about you.' He paused. 'No, that's wrong. Joanna, I love everything about you.'

He said it calmly, his voice steady, yet she saw his love in his eyes, heard it in his voice, felt it in the gentleness of his arms around her.

It resonated through his words. 'I love you more than I ever expected to be able to feel. I wouldn't face it because it scares me. I don't *want* to love anyone as your mother loved—it makes me feel totally out of control—but I can't help it. And each day it gets stronger.'

Coming like that, unexpectedly, after the happiest day of her life so far, his confession was infinitely precious. Her eyes filled with tears, and she stepped into his embrace, holding him fiercely. 'I love you too,' she said simply. 'I'll always love you.'

Much later, lying locked in his arms after coming totally apart in them, Jo heard him say, 'Happy now that you know it was me who made the chiefs the offer they couldn't refuse?'

'I knew the moment Meru told me,' she said simply.

'Did you, indeed?' He tilted her chin and subjected her to one of his unrelenting surveys. 'So when did you know you loved me?'

'When you came back from Shanghai.' Smiling, she turned her head and kissed his shoulder. 'You were watching the blackbird doing her usual operatic show of suspicion, and you were smiling and…well, I realised that what I was feeling had to be love.'

'So you agreed to marry me before you knew about my dealings with the Council of chiefs?' He moved a little restlessly. 'I'm not usually such a coward. I don't even know when I fell in love with you—it was a process, not a moment.'

She hugged him, replete with pleasure yet still able to thrill to the instant flexion of his muscles. 'I think that realisation is always part of a process, but I already knew before you told me,' she said demurely.

His chest rose and fell with silent laughter. 'How did you guess?'

'When we got married without any suggestion of signing a pre-nuptial agreement.'

'That's when I realised that you truly loved me too.' Luc laughed again before saying quietly, 'Thank you, Tom, wherever you are.'

'Amen,' Jo said.

And locked together, the soft sigh of the trade winds carrying the perfumes of the island to them, they slid into a sleep without cares or fears for the future.

* * * * *